THE BIG BRAND

The town of Wolf Bait, western Wyoming, held only bitter memories for Ashford Larkin. When he first arrived he had had reason and purpose in his life, and his saddle bags had been full of hope. Then his cattle had stampeded, he had been shot, and his pard had been killed. Now, all he had left was his courage. Larkin did not know for sure the identity of the sidewinder who'd set him up, but with a price on his head and vengeance in his heart, Larkin was set on the ultimate lead reckoning!

THE BIG BRAND

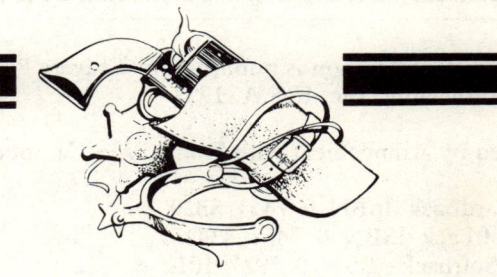

Orlando Rigoni

ATLANTIC LARGE PRINT
Chivers Press, Bath, England.
Curley Publishing, Inc.,
South Yarmouth, Mass., USA.

Library of Congress Cataloging-in-Publication Data

Rigoni, Orlando.
  The big brand / Orlando Rigoni.
    p.   cm.—(Atlantic large print)
  ISBN 0-7927-1012-6
  1. Large type books.   I. Title.
[PS3568.I374B5   1992]
813'.54—dc20

91-29707
CIP

British Library Cataloguing in Publication Data available

This Large Print edition is published by Chivers Press, England, and Curley Publishing, Inc, U.S.A. 1992

Published by arrangement with Donald MacCampbell, Inc.

U.K. Hardback ISBN 0 7451 8329 8
U.K. Softback ISBN 0 7451 8341 7
U.S.A. Softback ISBN 0 7927 1012 6

© Copyright 1972, by Lenox Hill Press

Photoset, printed and bound in Great Britain by
REDWOOD PRESS LIMITED, Melksham, Wiltshire

**Dedicated to:
NELLIE EZELL**

THE BIG BRAND

CHAPTER ONE

Ashford Larkin, his longish brown hair straggling below the brim of his warped Stetson, rode into the huddle of shacks that clung to the chattering waters of the Fontenelle ten miles above its marriage with the Green. Wolf Bait, the town was called, spawned and nurtured in the western edge of Wyoming. He'd been through the town before on his way to Denver with his modest herd of prime cattle. There had been reason and purpose in his life then, and his saddle bags had been full of hope. Now his brown eyes were devoid of joy, and his full-lipped mouth was a straight line above his lean jaw. His saddle bags were filled with hate, and in his broad chest burned the hell-fires of revenge. There were signs of winter creeping down off the Tetons, and the bullet still imbedded in his back was making its presence known with a dull persistence; a goad to remind him of a debt that had to be collected from a debtor he wasn't even sure of.

He rode up the twisting street past the millinery and dressmaking establishment, in the door of which stood a woman with a wealth of tawny hair, wearing a purple dress with a soft, turned-down collar. She had a pretty face, but one haunted by unrelished memories. He had tipped his hat to her on his former visit to town, and she had smiled at him. Vera Rand, the name in the corner of the display window had read. At the sight of him she raised a slim hand to her face, but she didn't smile. Perhaps his own grim countenance had precluded even a gentle recognition. Virgil Culp had been with him that last time, and now Virg was gone. The loss of his cattle had been disaster enough, but the violence visited upon Virg and himself had overshadowed it.

He doffed his hat to Vera Rand, and she nodded solemnly. Her expression seemed to say, 'I'm not looking at the same young man I smiled on before. The features are there, but inside the skin there's an older man; a bitter man.'

Ash gave her no cause to soften her posture. Through his mind flashed that night two months before. He and Virg had bedded their small herd for the night, a night faintly illuminated by a slivered moon. The night was calm, with no sign of anything that could spook the herd, so they both went to sleep confident the herd would remain on the bedding ground. The spook came in the form of catastrophe. A swarm of cattle bore down on them before they could get the sleep out of their eyes. They had only time to scramble out of the way of the sharp, pounding hooves of the juggernaut. They had managed to keep their guns and began firing at the herd, hoping to stop or divert it. Answering shots sliced at them through the dark. He had heard Virg cry out, 'I'm hit!' Then a bullet had hammered into his own back, and another had creased his skull, knocking him unconscious. (He fingered the red scar above his right ear where the hair had not yet grown back.) When he had come to, there was no sign of Virgil Culp, no sign of his cattle. His mouth was swollen from thirst, and pain wracked his body. He had no way of knowing how long he had lain in the bitter cold of night and the scorching heat of day. Fortunately for him, a trapper on his way to Fort Bridger found him and hauled him to the fort. It was to be two months before he could leave the infirmary at Fort Bridger.

When the gangrene had subsided and the poison had seeped from his system, he had been as weak as a cat, unable to stand on his own two feet. An Irish girl, Mary Flynn, wife of a sergeant at the fort, nursed him back to health, and now here he was, hollow-cheeked, raw-boned, but tough and eager for the trials he knew lay ahead. He was on his way back to Puma Valley, without money, cattle or Virgil Culp. If Virg had been able to travel, he would not have left him lying half dead and unprotected on the open trail. Whether or not Virg was dead he didn't know, but why Virg had deserted him was a riddle that would gnaw at him for the rest of his life.

He stopped before the two-story log building, the lime chinking in the walls giving it a skeletal look. The sign, swinging on the rusty bailing wire that held it over the door, read: 'First Chance.' He knew the opposite side of the sign read: 'Last Chance.' It was the only chance there was in the meager town except for Bootleg Charley's, which catered to the Indians and the riffraff who couldn't afford decent likker. He dallied his horse and went in through the three-inch-thick plank door which guarded the place against the periodic onslaughts of Indians and cow tramps who, half crazed with boot-leg hooch, hoped to find girls inside to fondle. Though he had been there on his way south, Ash was still amazed at the contrast on the inside of the sway-backed building. The walls were painted red with a pigment dug out of the earth. The sawdust, procured from the mill on the creek, was clean and sweet-smelling. The glasses on the back bar shone in the light of the bracket lamps, which were already lit. Gospel McKinley, the black barkeep, was the only person in the room. Leffa Hanks was nowhere in sight.

Ash Larkin shoved the battered Stetson back on his rusty head and scratched his ear. 'Whose funeral you fixed up for, Gospel?' Larkin mused.

'Reckon theah ain't no funeral, suh,

leastways not yet.'

Larkin took another look about the orderly place. 'Weddin' mebbe?'

'No weddin', suh.'

Larkin scowled. 'Where's Leffa?'

As though on cue, a woman appeared from a door at the end of the bar. She was a tall, angular woman with pantherish movements. Her hair, which had been blonde, was streaked with brown, and it framed her longish face with its straight strands, which were caught in a cluster of curls at the nape of her neck. Her hazel eyes were neutral; they had seen both sides of life's coin, the dirty and the clean.

'Hullo, pilgrim,' Leffa said in a sulky voice.

'You remember me?' Larkin said, his chin thrusting out.

'I remember a young buck full of eagerness and high hope, heading south with his partner to sell his cattle. I don't remember the name.'

'Larkin—Ash Larkin.'

'That's right. The name's the same, but the man isn't. I remember my girls took a fancy to you. What ran the meat off your bones—hard luck?'

'A man takes the hard with the soft, ma'am. Too much soft weakens a man.'

'And too much hard embitters him. A bitter man is a troublesome man, Larkin,'

Leffa mused, her mouth straight and her eyes locked on him.

'Riddle me not, ma'am. What's with all this stagnation 'round here? Where's the girls?'

'Upstairs waiting.'

'Waitin' for what? The second comin'?' Ash scowled. 'And the customers, they on a boycott?'

Leffa looked at the black man. 'Didn't you explain, Gospel?'

'Ah didn't have no time, Leffah. Reckon he didn't get the word.'

'What word?' Larkin snapped. 'You expectin' a Bible ranter here to save our souls? My throat's scratchy, my stomach's cravin', and my morale needs boostin'. I need me some redeye.'

'Go down to Bootleg Charley's.'

'You wouldn't condemn a man to death 'thout a hearin', would you? I ain't conditioned to rotgut; that takes persistence an' suicidal tendencies,' Larkin opined.

'Water the rotgut down and put some tabasco in it,' Leffa advised.

'Whyfore you rejectin' business, ma'am?'

'Quit calling me ma'am; you sound like a sheep. Sheep aren't popular around here. I'm Leffa Hanks or, as some of the smart alecks call me, Leftover.'

'You don't exactly look like a leftover, Hanks. Reckon if you'd let yore hair grow to its natural darkness to fit yore olive complexion, you'd be right handsome. Now bein' as this is a public place, I want that drink. It is a public place, ain't it?'

'For the moment, yes. Give him a drink, Gospel,' Leffa told the barkeep.

Just then a pickaninny girl stuck her head in the front door. 'They's comin' up the road, Missy Hanks!' the child cried in a shrill voice, and disappeared into the gathering gloom outside.

'You ain't enlightened me very much, Hanks. Who's comin'?'

'Drink your drink, pilgrim, and get out.'

'I ain't in no hurry. I aim to have me another one after this'n.'

'As I said, a bitter man is a troublesome man. There won't be any trouble if you leave. The Big brand outfit is coming on their way to the Hole. They make this their halfway stop. They're mighty fractious and thirsty when they get here. Now get out and save what meat is left on your bones.'

'You make me curiouser by the minute, Leftover.' He hadn't meant to use that name, but it had slipped out. 'There ain't no brand so big it can't be whittled down.'

'Is that what happened to you, Larkin?'

'No, ma'am. I was poleaxed.'

'What do you mean? What happened? Did your partner get killed?'

'My troubles are mine, Hanks. Ain't no

cause for you to be concerned. Whan did the Big outfit drive south?'

'About a week after you left here. They were hurrying to hit the top price market.'

There was a commotion outside; then the heavy door swung open and the Big outfit tramped in. They were led by a man who lived up to the brand. He was *big*. They were all big men, not a runt among them. The boss had a square, heavy-jawed face with ice-blue eyes looking out from under thin, scraggly eyebrows. He took his tall hat off his thick black hair, which formed a widow's peak in the center of his forehead. He looked at Leffa, who stood tall and quiet in her place.

'Well, Leffa, we're here!' he announced.

'Boris Bigge, anybody would have to be deaf, dumb and blind not to know that,' Leffa said without humor.

'Cheer up, honey. We ain't goin' to bust up nothin'. I'm buyin' your place, lock, stock and barrel, and I hope there's enough stock. How come you got a strange waddy in here? You was sent word this was Bigge night.'

Larkin tensed at the bar; he could smell trouble. So that was where the Big brand had got its name—Bigge. Bigge lived up to the name; he was a beefy man, broad in the shoulders but a little paunchy in the stomach. He pulled off his gauntleted gloves, exposing ham-like hands, as white as a woman's. Larkin, still not entirely recovered from his ordeal of physical violence, had misgivings about standing up to such a man. Bigge was six-two or more. Larkin knew he almost matched him in height, but poundage was another matter. Still, he didn't back down.

One of Bigge's riders, an outsized youngish man with shaggy hair and a flat-paned face, said with a grin, 'Want I should throw him out, boss?'

'Don't get edgy, Lundy,' Boris said to the man. 'Let the waddy finish his drink.'

Without looking up from his glass, Larkin said, 'I figgered on havin' me another after this.'

There was a disquieting silence. 'Ain't you heard of us Big boys?' another waddy spoke up. He had thick black hair and deep-sunken brown eyes.

Larkin looked up and turned his head to take in both ends of the bar. 'You're tol'able big, all right. Yeah, I heard of you. You followed me down the trail toward the railroad about two months ago. You was in a hurry.'

'So what?' Bigge scowled. His big nose, which showed signs of having been flattened more than once, twitched. 'What's your name, boy? You look kinda peaked.'

'Name's Larkin. The peakedness comes from a cause,' Ash said flatly.

'Are you carryin' Rocky Mountain tick fever, boy?'

'You might call it hog fever. Some outfit, big like yourn, stampeded through my camp, took my herd with it an' left me an' my buddy for dead.'

Uneasiness filled the room. 'You accusing me, Larkin?'

'I ain't named no names. Did you find any Slash-L cattle 'mongst your shipment at the check-off?'

'You ain't making pleasant conversation, Larkin. I sell only the brands I contracted for. My men keep whatever strays they pick up on the way.'

'Next he'll be wantin' to see our tally sheet,' Lundy said, his loose mouth showing big, uneven teeth.

Then another voice piped up, a high, shrill voice that triggered a subconscious memory in Larkin's brain. 'Let's finish him off an' get on with our business!'

Like the sear of a hot branding iron, that voice brought back the night of the stampede. After he and Virgil had shot to turn the herd, there had been a shout on the air, the only words spoken that night:

'Somebody's throwin' lead! Let's finish them off!'

That voice brought back all the fury, excitement and agony of that night. He felt an awareness of danger, but he dared not cut bait and run. To make any real charges here would be tantamount to suicide. Bigge himself dampened the danger.

'Give him his other drink, Gospel. I got business with Leffa.' He turned to Leffa, who had been watching with her dark hazel eyes. 'Where are the girls?'

'They're waiting upstairs—my orders,' Leffa said in her throaty voice with a touch of Southern drawl in it, 'until I make sure they're not going to be mistreated by your savages.'

'Leffa, why do you think I'm buyin' your place? I'm not buyin' the girls—you can handle them—I'm just buyin' the bar and the stock. Ain't none of my men goin' to destruct my property.' He turned to Lundy. 'Mitch, you gather up the guns and lock 'em in the beer cellar.' He turned back to Leffa. 'That satisfy you, honey?'

Leffa shrugged her bare shoulders. 'Come in the back, and we'll make out the papers, Boris.' To Gospel she said, 'Go upstairs and turn the girls loose.'

Larkin felt edgy and exposed without Bigge's discipline in the room, but the advent of the girls, coming down the stairs in their short, fancy dresses and permeating the air with heady perfume, shielded him for the moment. He turned his head to see if Michele Turner was among them. She was there, her dark mane flowing down her back. Then his attention was attracted by another girl, a black girl, who was as slim and fancy as the others. The Big men were puzzled by the innovation.

'Where in thunder did Leffa pick up the black sheep?' Lundy asked.

Michele Turner answered him. 'Leffa figures that too much white meat ain't good for a man.'

The men laughed at this. They showed a curiosity about the new girl, as there were few such in Wyoming. Michele, the prettiest and most responsive girl in the covey, saw Larkin and made straight for him.

'What happened to you, cowboy? You've lost a lot of meat.'

'Just my baby fat, Mike.' He had called her Mike the last time. 'I just growed up; painful process.'

'How come you're mixed up with the Bigge boys?'

'I ain't exactly mixed up with 'em. They're tryin' to sift me out, but I don't like to be shoved.'

'You look like you've been shoved plenty. There's no bubble in you any more. Last time you were full of glee. Buy me a drink?'

'I never refuse a lady. Gospel, tea for one,' Larkin said loudly enough for the others to hear.

'Don't listen to him, Gospel. You know my preference—my first of the evening is always real and raw. You might try one; it could cheer you up.'

'This is my allowance.' He indicated his drink. 'Finish this, I vamoose.'

'You being pressured?'

'Bigge pressure. He just bought the bar; it's his private club now.'

'He didn't buy me!' Michele said vehemently.

'He made a point of that.'

'Then come up to my room and drink.'

'There won't be no profit in it.'

'There are different kinds of profit, Ash. A nun finds profit in virtue.'

'You aimin' to be a nun?'

'I might have been one. Things didn't work out. I like you, Ash; you make a woman feel respectable.'

'Amen,' Ash said sanctimoniously. 'I don't know if I appreciate that compliment or not.'

Mitch Lundy had been listening to their conversation while talking to Beulah, the black girl. He swung around, put his long fingers on Larkin's arm and swung him away from the bar.

'You've had yore pap, cowboy; now slope! Quit annoyin' this gal; she's mine.'

Michele turned from the bar, fire in her dark eyes. She deliberately threw what was left of her drink into Lundy's face.

'I don't belong to you or anybody else, Mitch Lundy! You Big boys have small brains, like elephants. Come on, Larkin; come up to my room and tell me what euchred you. You've evidently been through hell.'

'Not half the hell he's going to be through if he don't get out of here!' Mitch snarled.

With one shove of his long arm, Mitch catapulted Larkin across the room. Ash, off balance, lost his footing. He slid on his rump across the floor and came up against the piano, parting with his gun and his hat in the process. For an instant the ignominy and the unfairness of the attack blinded him with a red haze. Before his eyes swam the night of the stampede and murder. He rose to his long legs and felt the rush of a cold and calculating fury drive him forward toward the man who had belittled him.

CHAPTER TWO

Lundy's open hand across Larkin's contorted face interrupted the charge, but not for long. Larkin beat the arm down with a savage chop. He landed a blow on Lundy's face, and Lundy, shocked by the swift riposte, snarled a curse and braced himself for a roundhouse swing. Larkin ducked under the wild blow and hammered two swift piston-like blows to Lundy's guts. Lundy grunted, swayed a little, and a killer mask slid over his rough-hewn features. Sobered by the swift and telling attack of the smaller man before him, Lundy shook back his wild hair and settled down to the business of butchery. The butchery was no one-sided affair. Ash kept his head down and smashed punches to Lundy's heart, his lean guts, the solar plexus. Lundy, wheezing and grunting from the punishment, beat Ash about the head and ears. The men in the room, realizing the affair was developing into a real fight, began making bets on the outcome. There were few takers against Lundy, but one of them was Michele Turner.

Lundy's weight and stamina began to tell; he had not been laid low for weeks with blood loss and fever. Ash felt himself weakening, his breath coming in broken sobs, his head bleary from the pummeling. He beat and battered Lundy's torso, but his strength was not equal to the task. He felt blood on his face, tasted it on his lips. He had to raise his attack. He had to hit Lundy on his square, ironhard jaw; hit him hard enough to knock him out. Ash braced himself, raised his head, and Lundy's big fist exploded in his face! Ash went down hard, but he didn't feel the sting of his rump hitting the sawdust floor. He shook his head. To lie there would be to invite the boot heel of the infuriated Mitch Lundy. Ash forced himself to his feet and threw punches at the square face that swam before him. There was blood on that square face, fury in the pale eyes and curses snarling from the cut lips. Mitch landed another blow with all the power of his big shoulder behind it. Ash was literally lifted off the floor. His head struck the floor as he fell. Stars danced before his eyes. He heard a roar go up from the men. Lundy was waiting like a panther to finish him off. Then, vaguely, he saw Michele behind Lundy. She lifted a bottle of whiskey above her dark head and smashed it upon Lundy's cranium!

A momentary hush went across the barroom as Lundy crashed down like a poleaxed ox. Into the vacuum of emotion, Bigge, with Leffa Hanks at his shoulder, strode into the room.

'What's going on here?' Bigge barked. 'I told you to let the pilgrim alone.'

'He was rough housin' the girls,' the man with the shrill voice charged.

'That's a lie!' Michele denied. 'He treated us proper. You wouldn't understand that, Jeff Alfora!'

Bigge looked at the two men lying on the floor. 'Throw some water over Lundy, and drag the pilgrim outside.'

Ash Larkin dimly heard what was going on. He felt hands dragging him and then the feel of the cool night air. He still had no will to get to his feet. Soft hands wiped the blood from his face, and he heard Michele's voice.

'Take his other arm, Beulah. We'll take

him into Vera's. She'll clean him up.'

Ash rose to his knees, then to his wobbly legs, with an angel of mercy on either side of him. He noticed that the hand on his left arm was the color of smooth, creamy chocolate. In the dim light of the storm lanterns that burned outside the Last Chance, he saw Michele's fair, solemn face.

'I've caused you a peck of trouble, Mike,' he lisped through bruised lips. 'Lundy ain't goin' to take kindly to bein' bashed in the head with a bottle. You girls are courtin' trouble sidin' me. Lead me to the first hoss trough an' throw me in.'

'Ah reckon we gals has faced trouble befoh,' Beulah said softly, 'specially mah kind. But even mean men has a bottom to theah meanness. Sometimes they's mean 'cause they's soft, an' afraid to show theah softness. Sometimes they's lonely, so lonely they even kiss a black gal like me. Mostly they need mothering.'

Ash heard the loneliness in the black girl's voice, but it was a loneliness tinged with hope. He wondered, in the back of his confused mind, just why she was at Leffa Hanks' place. Before he could guess at the reason, they led him into a softly lit place that smelled of satin and feathers and a subtle perfume.

'Bring him back here, Michele,' a quiet voice said.

'He's bruised and bloody, Vera.'

'That's all right. I heard the disturbance from here and saw them throw him out. You girls had better get back to your business; the men will resent your siding a pilgrim.'

When the girls had gone, Vera led Ash into a neat and spotless bedroom parlor that smelled of lye soap and the bouquet of sweet peas that graced the dresser. A picture of a man hung on one wall, a thin, sober man with a string tie and dark hair parted precisely in the middle of his forehead. It could not be Vera's husband; he was too old.

'Ma'am, you're goin' to a mess of trouble for a total stranger.'

'You're not a stranger, except—'

'Except what?'

'The last time when you rode out, you were a man of flesh and humor. You smiled at me.'

'An' you smiled back. Reckon I didn't see no smile when I rode in, ma'am.'

'Call me Vera. The sight of you sobered me. Tragedy marks a man.'

'And a woman, Vera. We all have our private tragedies; sometimes we nurture them, and sometimes we destroy them.'

'Or they destroy us, Ash Larkin.'

'You know my name,' he charged, surprised.

'I made it a point to find out. You're no man of flesh and humor now, Ash; you're a man gaunted and bedeviled. But no matter;

lie down and let me fix you.'

'Reckon I cain't, Vera, not on that satin counterpane. Like I told the girls, steer me to the nearest water trough an' throw me in,' Ash told her.

'All right, be stubborn. Sit up, then—' she indicated an oaken rocker—'and let me take off your shirt.'

'My shirt stays,' he said adamantly.

'It's bloody.' She proceeded to unbutton his shirt in spite of his protests.

His broad chest, gaunted from the rash of fever, showed bones through the matted hair. He subdued his objections because, as Beulah had said, he was one of the lonely ones, and he needed mothering. He submitted to her ministrations, savoring the warm, clean smell of her. Her small hands worked gently but quickly, cleansing away the blood from his face and his chest. She brought him a clean shirt which he accepted without remonstrance, and he wondered if the man on the wall had at one time worn it. The proceedings were interrupted by the arrival of Gospel's little girl, who had warned of the coming of the Big outfit.

'You need me, Missy Vera?' Cleo piped up.

'Go fetch Blacky Brown for me, Cleo.'

'Sho'nuff, ma'am. I reckon he won't be too drunk yit.'

'Take the back road to his cabin, Cleo, and don't stop at Bootleg Charley's. Understand?'

'Yes'm, I understand, Missy Vera.'

The child, with her pigtails and red ribbons, disappeared into the darkness, and Larkin was perturbed at the danger she was being subjected to on his account.

'Vera, I don't like this a-tall,' he objected. 'You're puttin' the child in jeopardy on my account. Reckon I can paddle my own canoe.'

'Cleo is in no danger. She's considered bad luck, like a black cat; nobody will harm her.'

'What's this about her stoppin' in Bootleg Charley's place?'

'She goes there and sings sometimes. The men throw her money—what little they can spare. Charley gets the hard-luck crowd.' She paused for a moment and then said, 'I'd fix you something to eat, but there won't be time. Bigge's crew will get noisier and rowdier the more they drink. There won't be any shooting, because Boris won't allow it, but they can rough up the town real good. You'd be prize bait for them. They won't look for you at Blacky Brown's. He's a queer duck. Not crazy queer, but foxy and knowledgeable. He'll do what I ask him.'

'I'm beholden to you, Vera. Yore man on the wall there must have been mighty proud of you when he was alive,' Ash hazarded.

'He's still alive,' Vera said enigmatically.

At Charley's cabin, to which he had been led by the old-timer, Ash was greeted by the smell of a bubbling pot filling the air with the promise of good eating. Charley had retrieved Ash's horse from the front of the Last Chance, and they had departed from the back door of Vera's place without being accosted. Blacky's cabin was neat and clean, the puncheon floor having recently been swabbed meticulously. The room was about sixteen feet square, with clinked log walls, a pine board table, some benches, and jerky hanging from the rafters. It was a snug haven.

'I got some slum b'ilin' on the stove, Larkin. From the looks of you, you could use some,' Blacky said.

Ash relished the stew of elk meat, potatoes, carrots and onions. His appetite assuaged, Ash rolled a quirly and leaned back in his chair.

'What do you do for a livin', Blacky? You reek of prosperity.'

Blacky Brown shrugged his round shoulders. 'I reckon I was finagled by the fickle finger of Fate, pardner.'

'Meanin' what?'

'Wal, hit's like this. Fust off I had me a gold prospect over yonder in the side of a hill near Cody. I hit me some pay dirt an' was prosperin' right well when I blasted smack into an underground stream o' water. The water filled my tunnel so I couldn't scrabble for gold no more. I was plumb flabbergasted fer a spell, figurin' how I could use the water. The stream ran into a natural basin, which I dammed up by blastin' muck into the small openin'. Purty soon I had myself a lake, not big, but sizable. One night I had a dream how to cash in with no capital an' no expenses. Beaver hats was becomin' right popular, an' beaver was gittin' scarce. I dreamed that cat fur would make a good substitute. But cats had to eat, an' a bright idee came to me.

'I stocked the lake with fish—catfish, savvy? Fish beget offspring at a surprisin' rate. Then I scrabbled around for cats, any kind of cats, an' I built cages for 'em. Cats likewise multiply fast, jest like fish. Purty soon I had jest the right balance o' cats an' fish. Then I was in a pure profit business.'

'Ain't no pure profit business,' Ash said, thinking of his lost herd.

'They was the way I worked it. You see, I fed the fish to the cats. Then I skinned the cats, sold the pelts an' fed the meat to the fish. So the fish was supportin' the cats, an' the cats was supportin' the fish. I was gittin' the hides for my trouble.'

'So that's how come you prospered, eh?' Ash mused.

'Nope. I prospered for a time, but then Fate finagled me some more. My pond began gittin' some black greasy stuff in the water. I couldn't figger it out. That greasy stuff was pure poison for the fish; they up an' died. I couldn't do nothin' but turn the cats loose. There I was, wonderin' what to do next. I thought I could bottle the greasy water an' sell it for medicine, but nobody could drink the danged stuff. I tried usin' it fer liniment, but it left my hide streaked with black that nothin' would get off but whiskey. I ain't a man to waste good likker cleanin' my hide.'

'Amen,' Ash intoned, amused by the oldster's story. 'You were the victim of Fate once more. But what about the prosperity?'

'Fate didn't desert me. I reckon she was jest testin' me. One day a Eastern dude who had lost his way stopped at my cabin. I told him about my pond, an' he went out an' looked at it. He felt the black, stinkin' stuff with his fingers, an' tasted it. He got real excited. He said the stuff was petrolatum, a black stuff they was diggin' for in Pennsylvania. They made lamp oil out of it, an' liniment, an' axle grease. To make a long story short, we made a deal. We drained the lake, the dude put up money to drill a well, an' to this day I'm gittin' a percentage of the profit he makes when the oil is refined.'

'Blacky, you was born in the lap of fortune. So far I ain't been nothin' but fortune's stepchild.' He told Blacky Brown about his experience on the trail, the loss of his partner Virgil Culp, and his long recuperation at Fort Bridger.

'I don't know for sure who the men were who bushwhacked us, but I got my suspicions,' he finished his story.

'What you aimin' to do?'

'Get back at 'em some day. I reckon I don't know how. I got some range, a meager ranch, but no money an' no cattle.'

'Mebbe I can help you, Larkin. It depends on how bad you want revenge, and what kind o' guts you got,' Blacky told him.

'I want revenge. My guts will have to prove themselves.'

'You know how Bigge operates?'

'Some.'

'He drives cattle for three outfits in the Hole. He keeps his Big outfit together by bein' generous to his men with other people's propity. Every trail outfit loses some cattle, but they pick up all the strays they can along the way. Bigge lets his men keep the strays an' divide the money from their sale among them.'

'I heard about that.'

'The Big outfit got into Wolf Bait the day after you pulled out. They knowed you was ahead of 'em. Drowsin' at a table in the Last Chance, I was close to some of Bigge's boys, who was playin' cards an' talkin'. I heard 'em talkin' about yore herd. Lundy said, "Supposin' we was to come upon that herd at night? We just might gobble it up an' dare Ash to try an' get 'em back." I reckon that's what they done, but they didn't mention killin',' Blacky said.

'We started the shootin',' Larkin said

ruefully. 'If I knew who murdered Virg, I'd kill him like a dog. They didn't even come back to see if we was hit.'

'Revenge delayed is made sweeter by the waitin',' Brown cautioned. 'You need money for a stake, right?'

'You either buy cattle or you steal 'em,' Ash grunted. 'I ain't a thief.'

'There's one quick way of makin' a stake, lad.'

'What's the magic word?'

'Sheep.'

Ash felt himself cringe instinctively at the word. 'You mean sheep in the Hole? It's crazy!'

'But possible. There's range around Jackson Hole fit only for sheep, but the cattlemen would die for that range rather than see sheep inhabit it.'

'Your arguments's without substance, Blacky. If I did consider it, where would I get the sheep?'

'Jim Thorson.'

'Don't know him.'

'He's big in the sheep business in Idaho around Targhee. He's lookin' fer range over this way, I've heard. I reckon he'll back any man with guts enough to invade the hole with woolies.'

'Blacky Brown, you know what that would mean?'

'A fight, I reckon.'

25

'A range war. For that you need money, men and muscle. The first herd to invade wouldn't get beyond Snow Mountain,' Ash said grimly.

'Thorson will supply all three. He's got the money, he kin buy you fightin' men, and for muscle he's got a hundred thousand sheep. Bigge an' his backers can't kill 'em all. He wants a toehold in Wyoming.'

'Why pick Jackson Hole?'

'It ain't the Hole he's interested in primarily. Don't you see? If he gets a clincher on the Hole, even a precarious clincher, the ranchers will be willin' to see him pick range jest outside the hole, like east of the Togwotee Pass, or even in Puma Valley,' Brown explained.

'Just a minute, old-timer. I ain't never give a thought to sheep.'

'Larkin, you're either a fool or a coward, an' I don't take you to be the latter. You say you're burnin' for revenge on the crew that euchred you. You likewise say you need a stake to make a new start. I'm suggestin' a way you can get both wishes, an' you're balkin' over the smell of an animal. You can get used to sheep smell oncet yore pocket is jinglin'.'

'How come you know so much about this here Jim Thorson an' his ambitions?' Ash queried.

'I talked to him in Idaho Falls, that new

settlement on the Snake. He wanted me to ramrod a herd into no-sheep land. I didn't need the dinero, and I had no vengeance in my soul.'

'I don't know nothin' about herdin' sheep. I'd lose 'em all to coyotes an' mountain lions, not to speak of Blackfeet an' Shoshones.'

'Thorson will supply the Basques, the camp wagons, the dogs and the provender. He'll also furnish a camp tender,' Brown explained.

'What's a camp tender?'

'The sayin' is that a sheepherder is crazy, but a camp tender is a sheepherder with his brains kicked out. He does like it says—tends camp, cooks the meals, butchers the meat, feeds the dogs an' gathers wood fer the stove. He's also company fer the herder.'

'Reckon I don't need that kind of company,' Ash objected.

'Not fer you, pardner. The Basque usually has his own kid in camp, or a mestizo he picks up somewhere. They sleep in a bed with rawhide laces an' a real mattress. You couldn't stand that. You tough cowboys have to sleep on the ground an' eat at a chuck wagon.'

'A chuck wagon for one man?' Ash queried.

'You're dumber than a bull on loco weed. You won't be one man; you'll have gunnies an' scouts to lead the way an' discourage the

27

opposition.'

'I'll have to sleep on it, Blacky,' Ash said dubiously.

He took the upper bunk that was built in one corner of the cabin, shucking the borrowed shirt that had belonged to a man close to Vera Rand; a man who was still alive. He crawled beneath the blankets with the blat and jangle of a sheep herd going through his head. Just as he drowsed off, he heard a shot in a distant part of the town.

CHAPTER THREE

In the morning Larkin was solemn as he ate the side meat and eggs Brown cooked for breakfast. Even the pungent smell of the coffee failed to titillate his spirit.

Ash was determined to go into town after breakfast in spite of Brown's advice to wait until the Big brand men had cleared out.

'I ain't skulkin' behind the skirts of a woman an' the hospitality of an old man, Blacky. I aim to walk the street free an' peaceable, takin' only what trouble is forced on me.'

'What about the proposition I mentioned last night?'

'You mean the woolies? I'm badgering that idea right now. Before I make a decision, I've got to look over the country real good. I ain't never conjured with the thought of sheep an' cattle living within smelling distance of each other.'

'I reckon a man makes his own plays, win, lose or draw. I figger you fer a man who would win or die, Larkin.'

'A dubious compliment,' Ash mused. 'I ain't ready to die.'

'Then go out an' win!'

Gun strapped to hip and tied to thigh, Larkin took his horse from Brown's stable and rode uptown. His lean face still smarted from the cuts and bruises Lundy had given him. His hat was tipped over his brown eyes against the glare of the morning sun. The town was strangely peaceable, Bigge's men no doubt sleeping off their convulsions of the night before. The door to Vera's shop was open, so he dismounted and went inside to thank her for the shirt and assure her he would replace it. Vera, behind the counter, greeted him with alarm on her face, while she pushed back the wayward strands of her light brown hair.

'I was afraid of this. Why did you come here now, Ash? Why didn't you wait for things to settle down?'

'Things never settle down, Vera. They just pause to catch their breath. I came to tell you I'll replace this shirt, for which I'm beholden.'

She reached under the counter and brought out his own shirt, washed and ironed. 'Here, take your shirt, and keep that other one,' she said.

'Reckon I can't do that, ma'am.' He changed shirts right in front of her and laid a dollar bill on the one she had loaned him. 'For the washin' and ironin',' he said evenly.

'Stubborn.' She sighed. 'You're walking into trouble, Ash Larkin.'

'I ain't never walked out of it,' Ash retorted.

'One of Bigge's men was shot and killed last night,' she said flatly.

Ash scowled. He remembered the shot he had heard just before dropping off to sleep. 'What's that got to do with me?' he queried.

'You ask that after what happened last night? You were beaten and booted. You disappeared. You naturally wanted revenge,' she pointed out.

'But I was in Blacky Brown's cabin all night. He can prove it.'

'If they give him a chance. Even then they wouldn't believe him; they think he's touched in the head. You could have slipped out during the night without waking Blacky.'

'Not when that shot was fired. I heard it just before I dropped off to sleep.' He pulled on one of his ears. 'How come there ain't more commotion in town, if they're lookin' for a killer?'

'The Big bunch were too busy rousting the town and making noise to hear the shot, or care about it if they did hear it.'

'Boris warned about trouble. He took their guns away,' Ash hazarded.

'He didn't confiscate the guns at Bootleg Charley's.' She added, 'Jasper Cole, the marshal, was in to see me. He's the only one knows about the killing. He didn't want to spread the news around with the Big crew liquored up. Whiskey and lynching make cozy bedfellows.'

'What did he want here?'

'He wanted to know where you went after you left here.'

'And you told him?'

'No. I didn't want it to get out you were at Brown's cabin. I was afraid Lundy might go after you. I told Jasper I didn't know where you went. I see now that was a mistake,' Vera acknowledged ruefully.

'A kind mistake, Vera. Don't fret.'

He left Vera's, a new wariness taking hold of him. He led his horse up to the Last Chance, dallied him to the rail and went inside. Gospel McKinley was behind the bar, straightening up the mess and confusion of the night before. Cleo was standing on a stool, polishing glasses. Leffa Hanks sat at one of the tables, her long face cupped in her hands. Ash sat down across from her.

'You're just the man to make my day

complete, Ash Larkin,' she said glumly.

'Glad to oblige, Leffa,' he quipped, knowing her meaning. 'Are you workin' for Bigge regular now?'

'Of course not.'

'He bought the bar.'

'He buys the bar every time they come through here. When they go, he sells it back to me for more than he paid to make up for loss and damage. It's his peculiar way of keeping down trouble. He opines that his men know better than to damage or destroy his property. Did you hear about the killing?'

'I heard the shot just before I dropped off to sleep at Blacky Brown's cabin. It ain't none of my affair.'

'Don't be too sure about that; you're the prime suspect. If I were you I'd slope on out of town.'

'And be tagged a hound dog? I'm the injured party; my cows stolen, my friend killed, and myself exterminated,' Ash said grimly.

'That's what makes you a prime suspect, including the beating you gave Mitch Lundy.'

'I took a beatin' myself. It would have been worse if it hadn't been for Michele Turner,' Ash reminded her.

The door to Leffa's quarters opened, and Michele came through. Ash took one look at her and felt a burning knot form in the pit of his stomach. Her pretty face was bruised, her lips cut, and one eye purple and swollen. A choking fury gripped him, and the urge to kill the man who had mishandled her made his hands tremble.

'Did I hear my name?' Michele said through her swollen lips.

'What in God's name happened to you, Mike?' Ash demanded.

'Lundy didn't stay unconscious as long as I thought he would. He decided I needed a lesson in manners.'

Larkin felt guilt and remorse.

'I'll kill the buzzard!' he said.

'Easy, Ash,' Michele cautioned. 'I was to blame. No man enjoys getting hit over the head with a whiskey bottle.'

'But you did it for me, Mike,' Ash insisted. 'There ain't no lady takin' a beating on my account without I mark or cripple the man who done it. It's a pure righteous truth.'

'Forget about righteousness; it's a doubtful commodity. Do me a favor, Ash, and let the matter lie,' Michele pleaded.

Leffa interposed, 'If Boris shows up, let me handle him.'

'Why? You women are wet-nursin' me like I was a snot-nosed kid,' Ash said. 'Want I should hide under yore skirt, Leffa?'

'I want you should get out of town alive, cowboy. You seemed determined to make it otherwise. I can handle Boris because he's got a yen for me; he wants to marry me.'

'Then why don't you marry him?' Ash snapped.

'I might have to to save your hide.'

'Oh, no, you don't! I ain't havin' no thoroughbred hitched up to a jackass on my account,' Ash proclaimed.

'Which one's the jackass, cowboy?' Leffa asked solemnly.

'You'd be a jenny, Leffa, not a jackass,' Ash reminded her.

'Thanks for letting me sleep in your room, Leffa,' Michele said.

'You'll sleep there until the Big brand bullies have gotten out of town. Boris will be here soon to sell me the bar back. Why don't you two disappear?'

Fate interceded. The heavy plank door creaked open, and Boris Bigge strode into the room, his square face as sour as vinegar. His spade hands were clenched, and his mouth was a slit above his jutting chin. He looked at them in turn, his eyes coming to rest on Larkin.

'Have you heard about my man, Stenner, getting killed?' he said grimly.

'He probably deserved it,' Leffa broke in. 'He was a mean one after the third or fourth drink.'

'He was unarmed, Leffa,' Boris said. 'I had him disarmed; that makes me partly responsible for his death. Killing an unarmed man is pure murder.'

'Have you got a suspect, Boris?'

'As good as needed. A shaggy-haired younker, making charges and with revenge in his heart for wrongs he can't prove, is fair game.'

'Whatever charge I made I'll one day prove, Bigge,' Ash said calmly.

'You might not have that one day, boy. My men are sleeping off their stupidity. I haven't told them what happened. I've advised Jasper Cole to lie on it for the time being, because I don't want a lynch party. Feeling mean from their hangovers, my men might try to top off their celebration with a rope. They might also hang the wrong man, especially with Lundy to prod them. Better come over to the jail, Larkin, and have Jasper lock you up. It will give you time to prove you had nothing to do with the shooting.'

Larkin almost felt the rope tightening about his throat. If the Big men had stolen his herd and killed Virg, they would relish hanging him to get rid of possible trouble. To run would be an admission of guilt.

'Do as he says, Ash,' Leffa instructed him.

'I reckon the jail might be a trap as well as a haven,' he objected.

'There's only one door, and the walls are adobe three feet thick,' Leffa assured him.

'Keep your gun if you're fretful,' Bigge offered, 'but use it only to save your life.'

'Thank you kindly, Bigge,' Ash said with

mock gravity.

'I'll send Cleo over with some dinner at noon,' Leffa said.

The jail cell was clean enough, though it had packed earth for a floor and a plank ceiling covered with baked clay. The blankets on the cot had been washed, and the adjoining cell was in the same unused condition. Larkin felt constrained to question Jasper Cole, the marshal. Cole was a man with a serious face, a thin pointed nose, and jowls that sagged from his long jaw. The two cells faced right on the marshal's office, so conversation was easy.

'For the mornin' after a night of hell-raisin', yore jail is in a mighty virginal condition, Marshal,' Ash opined.

'I've got a truce with Boris. His men have the run of the town while here. Bigge pays all damages an' takes it outa the men's pay.'

'Does he pay for murder, too?'

'It was his man got killed. Boris takes the guns from his men.'

'Ain't you ever heard of a cowboy havin' a extra gun in his warbag, Marshal?'

'There's a lot of things I've heard I pay no attention to. From what we got to go on, Stenner was murdered.'

'It could have been a fair fight, Cole. Stenner could have flashed a hideout gun.'

'That will have to be proved at the hearing,' Jasper Cole informed him.

36

'If there is a hearin', Marshal. Lynch mobs don't listen to no reason 'cept their own. Have you sent for Blacky Brown yet?'

'I reckon Leffa took care of that. She's on your side. She sent the pickaninny to fetch him. Too bad you haven't got a more reliable witness.'

'He's the only witness I got. How you goin' to have a trial here? There ain't no judge,' Ash reminded him.

'It will be a hearing, not a trial. If we get a likely suspect, we'll send him to Fort Bridger and let the judge-advocate take care of him.'

'You mean the suspect will face a kangaroo court if he reaches Bridger alive,' Ash jeered.

'I'll deliver you personally,' Cole said calmly.

'Not me, you won't. I ain't guilty.'

'Save it for the hearing, Larkin.'

'You put Lundy on the stand, and I'll be lied into hell,' Ash declared bitterly.

Ash sat on the slat-bottomed cot, his mind busy with his plight. No matter what he did or which way he moved, trouble seemed to hug him to her bosom.

Before long there was a commotion outside. Somebody hollered for the marshal. 'Okay, Marshal, keep out of our way an' you won't get hurt. Ain't no sense wastin' time on a trial fer that man you got in there!' It was Jeff Alfora's high-pitched voice, the voice Ash remembered from the stampede.

Jasper Cole rose to his tall height; he had the ramrod-stiff bearing of an officer and a gentleman. He took a shotgun from the rack on the wall and strode toward the barred door. Calmly he took the bar from the brackets.

'Tell them I've got my gun with me,' Ash suggested.

Cole gave no sign that he heard. He swung the door back and stood in the opening, facing the knot of men gathered in the dusty street.

'Did I hear somebody call me?' he said cryptically.

'You heard right, Marshal. We want the prisoner,' Mitch Lundy said, his face still bruised and cut from the fight of the night before. 'No sense wasting time on him. We'll grant him the law of the *refugio* like they give the Mexicans down in Sonora. Let him run like a coyote, an' if we don't kill him and he gets away, he's free.'

Ash shouted loudly enough for the men to hear. 'Lundy, I'll take you on any time for what you done to Michele! Only a yellow-livered skunk would treat a woman like that!'

'I was drunk,' Lundy yelled back, 'and dazed from bein' hit over the head with the bottle. Some women enjoy a beating!'

'You mean some skunks enjoy beatin' up a defenseless woman!'

'Go away, you men. We'll have a hearing this afternoon to decide if the prisoner is a plausible suspect,' Cole said.

'Plausible?' Lundy snorted. 'He's made threats against the Big. Somehow in his cotton brain he figgers we stole his cattle and killed his friend. Don't that make a man a plausible suspect? We're comin' in after him, Cole.'

'This is the only hole big enough to crawl through in this jail, men. If you come through here, you'll have to come through me. If you do come through me, some of you will die. Larkin has his gun on him.'

'What? What kind of a jail you runnin', Marshal, letting the prisoners have guns? Bigge won't like this.'

'It was Boris Bigge's idea, Lundy.'

That silenced them for a minute. 'One of our waddies was killed last night, Cole. We ain't passin' that up as a minor occurrence. Us Big men stand together, come hell or high water. If one of us gets killed with no quick action in rebuttal, then others of us will die. We got enemies same as everybody, but we exterminate our enemies to keep the proddy ones quiet,' Lundy declared.

'Come on, Lundy; let us make pronto weeth the rope,' a dark bony-faced man spoke up.

'All right, Tony Salazar, you want to make

the first try?' Cole taunted. 'Bigge wants no lynching.'

'Bigge ain't the law, *señor*. There ees one law above all the others, *amigo*; the law of the *diente* and the *clavo*, the tooth and the nail. All justice narrows down to thees, *señor*, among men or among armies. Boris Beege cannot change thees law.'

Just at that moment Boris strode before the group, his beefy shoulders hunched and his square face a storm cloud. His peaked Stetson made him look even taller than his six-foot-two.

'I'm changing that law right now, Salazar. There'll be no lynching. Men have dropped their fangs and clipped their nails to be different from animals. We'll have the hearing and abide by the results.'

'This killing is a knife in the belly of the Big brand, boss,' Lundy objected.

'A belly stab ain't usually fatal, Lundy. The Big brand can stand it for a spell. Go get some fodder in your guts and black coffee, savvy. No lacing in the java. Sober up. We're pushin' on right after the hearing.'

'Before or after the hangin'?' Jeff Alfora inquired.

'The hanging will be at Fort Bridger, Alfora. If you're aimin' to be present, better draw your pay now and head for the fort,' Bigge informed him without humor.

Grumbling, the men turned toward the Mesquite Cafe to humor their stomachs and settle their minds. Through the open door, Ash watched them go.

CHAPTER FOUR

The hearing was held in Jasper Cole's office, the only building in town that could be dignified with the title of courthouse. Cole, acting as judge, sat behind his desk in the corner of the room. What chairs were available were lined up against the far wall, occupied by the first-comers, mostly the crew of the Big brand. Ash found himself confined to his cell, to be tried behind the safety of the bars. Evidently Cole didn't trust the Big men, making sure they could not capture the prisoner by force if the trial didn't suit them. Ash looked at the hostile group, but there was no sign of Blacky Brown. It would be a lopsided trial: his word against the word of the men who would like to see him eliminated. One thing puzzled him. Boris Bigge wasn't there, pointing the fact that Bigge, like Pontius Pilate, was washing his hands of the execution. With not one witness on his side, it amounted to an execution.

Then a strange thing happened. The women of Wyoming, who had lately gained the right to vote, asserted themselves. Leffa Hanks was there, a velvet bonnet lined in white covering her streaky hair. Michele Turner, a white dress buttoned to her throat to hide what bruises it could, was at Leffa's side. The bruises on Michele's soft, beautiful face were mute evidence of the character of the witnesses for the state. The black girl, dressed in her fancy working clothes, was right behind them with Cleo.

'We come as witnesses for the defense, Marshal,' Leffa said boldly.

There was a moment of hush in the room, and then four of the men on the chairs let chivalry overcome prejudice. They rose, doffed their hats and gave their seats to the women.

Cole cleared his throat. 'This hearing will now come to order. Who's acting for the state?' He looked at Mitch Lundy.

'I reckon we expected Boris Bigge to make charges, Marshal.' Lundy looked at the women. 'Where's Bigge?'

'He was detained by unforeseen circumstances, Jasper,' Leffa said flatly.

Ash, his eyes on Michele, saw her give him a covert wink. It suggested collusion of some sort, but he couldn't imagine what.

'In Bigge's absence, I recognize myself as witness for the state,' Lundy said. 'I'm next in charge.'

'State your case, Mister Lundy.'

'It's a open an' shut case, Marshal. The suspect had the misfortune to lose his herd to some longropers a couple of months ago on the trail to Denver. There was some shootin'. His pardner was apparently shot and disappeared. The suspect comes into town, blamin' the Big brand for his troubles. He stirs up a quarrel on Mister Bigge's private property, an' then refuses to migrate when he is warned of trespass. He started manhandlin' the gals, an' I stepped in to argue with him. He got beat up an' booted out. Then he disappeared. He was stalkin' the town for revenge, an' he came across the deceased, a Mister Stenner, employed by Boris Bigge...'

There was a slight commotion as Vera Rand entered the room and took the seat that had been vacated by Lundy when he arose to make his speech. Vera wore a dress with a shawl collar that matched her eyes.

Lundy went on with his speech. 'And confronting Mister Stenner, the suspect did with malice aforethought and felonious intent—'

'Watch yore language, Lundy!' Ash called out. 'There's women present!'

Lundy gave him a dirty look, but he finished his verbose sentence with grim determination ignoring the ripple of laughter that spread across the room '—shoot and kill Mister Stenner, an unarmed man.'

'That's a lie!' Ash denied.

'You won't have no thought of women once you're danglin' from a rope,' Lundy growled.

He almost sat on Vera's lap, but caught himself and gave her a curt look as he backed up against the wall.

'You'd better make sure I hang, Lundy. I ain't got no stomach for woman beaters.'

Cole rapped for order with the butt of his gun. 'Enough of this levity,' he cautioned. 'A man's life is at stake here. Are there any more witnesses for the state? Any eyewitnesses?'

Tony Salazar, with tangled black hair and a hawkish face, spoke up. 'I seen the hombre in the cage runnin' away from the shootin', Marshal.'

A hush followed that damning evidence. Ash objected again. 'That's a danged lie, Marshal. He didn't see me no place. I'm bein' framed proper.'

'Shut up, Larkin, unless you want to defend yourself,' Cole warned.

'I ain't got nobody else to defend me,' Ash said bitterly.

'Any more witnesses for the state?' Cole asked.

'We aren't a state yet, Marshal; we're a territory.' Leffa reminded him.

'Quit splitting hairs,' Cole rapped. 'Any more witnesses for the prosecution?'

'What more do you want?' Lundy said. 'You got a eyewitness.'

'Yo'all have got a bald-faced liah, Jedge,' Beulah spoke up. 'Tony Salazar waz at the Last Chance all evenin'!'

'Who's callin' who a liar?' Tony retorted. 'I can prove I wasn't. You can ask the trail tramps over at Bootleg Charley's.'

'Reckon that's mostly right, Judge,' a short, whiskered man with walking-beam shoulders, said from one side of the room. 'I'm Charley. He was at my place, but I didn't keep an eye on him all night. He could have gone out for a breather. My joint gets foul at times; there ain't no windows.'

'Does the prosecution rest?' Cole asked, staring at the Big men.

'Hell, yes! Let's have the verdict, Jasper. We ain't got all day. Reckon if Bigge was here, he'd finish this up quick and tight,' Lundy growled.

'Are there any witnesses for the defense?'

'I'm a witness for the defense,' Leffa said, rising to her feet.

'I want no more perjury,' Cole warned.

Leffa tried to take suspicion off Larkin, but without perjuring herself, she could give little convincing testimony that Ash had not fired the shot.

Beulah, having once lied, was willing to try again. 'Reckon I heard that Mistah Salazar talkin' about shootin' somebody.'

'This black girl ain't got no right to testify in this court, Cole. She ain't a proper citizen,' Lundy protested.

'Ah's jest as much a propah citizen as yo'all, Mistah Lundy. Mistah Lincoln made me a citizen with his 'mancipation proclivities. Ah can vote in this territory.'

Vera rose. 'I'm speaking in the defense of Mister Larkin. He was brought into my place beaten and half conscious. I took care of him and sent Cleo for Blacky Brown, who took him to his cabin where he could keep out of trouble.'

'Did you see him arrive at Brown's cabin, Miss Rand?' Cole queried.

'It's *Missus* Rand,' Vera corrected him.

Ash, his heart going out to the women who were trying to help him, heard the correction and remembered the picture on her wall.

'All right, Missus Rand. Did you see him arrive at the cabin?'

Vera hesitated. 'No,' she said in a small voice.

'I did, I did,' Cleo piped up, raising her small black hand. 'I followed him an' Blacky to the cabin. Aftah that I stopped at Bootleg Chahley's to sing foh money.'

'Alone?' Jasper Cole queried, frowning.

'Of couhse, Yoh Honah. Ain't nobody harmin' me, even touchin' me. Ah's taboo, bad luck, that's me.' Cleo grinned. 'Made mahself foh dollah an' eighty cents.'

'Is this true?' Cole glowered at Charley.

'I reckon she was there, Marshal,' Charley agreed.

Cole turned back to Cleo. 'Did you see them go into the cabin?'

'They went to the bahn to put up their hosses.'

'And then?'

'I didn't see no more of 'em. I figgahed they went in the back doh.'

'Such evidence is inconclusive,' Cole said. 'This is merely a hearing. It has produced no proof of innocence or guilt. Mister Salazar claims to have seen Ashford Larkin running away from the scene of the crime. If that be perjury, it can be dealt with at the proper time. I have no recourse but to hold Ashford Larkin in custody and deliver him to Fort Bridger for trial.'

A hush went over the room. Jeff Alfora broke the silence. 'I got a feelin' he ain't never goin' to reach the fort, Marshal.'

There was another moment of silence. Ash knew he was in deadly danger.

This time the silence was broken by Michele Turner, who stood up in her white dress and looked about with her battered face. Ash wondered what testimony she had that might help him. She had not seen him after leaving him at Vera's.

'Marshal Cole, while this court is in session and all the townspeople are here to witness my plea, I wish to bring a charge of assault and battery against Mitch Lundy,' Michele lisped clearly through swollen lips.

A surge of excitement crossed the room.

'He did *that* to you?'

'I have plenty of witnesses to prove it.'

Mitch jumped away from the wall and croaked, 'You bring charges of assault and battery against *me*? What about the bottle you broke over my head?'

'That was to prevent a murder,' Michele said, looking him straight in the eye.

'You got no witnesses I beat you; I done it in your own room!' Mitch croaked, incriminatinmg himself.

'You were the only one in my room, and you were seen to come out. I hope you're proud of yourself, woman beater!' Michele charged.

There was a restless movement across the room, and all eyes were on Mitch Lundy. Mitch, finding himself in the role of the accused, squirmed uneasily.

'We ain't here to try me; we're here to try Larkin!' Lundy barked, hoping to get the trial back in focus.

But it didn't get back into focus. Into the room came a young girl, her eyes red from weeping and her torn dress held together by safety pins. Behind her walked her mother, and following them came Blacky Brown! The commotion in the room calmed down as they stared at the new actors in the drama.

'What's this intrusion all about, Mister Brown?' Jasper Cole inquired sternly.

'That's the fust time I been called *mister* in long time, Jedge,' Brown opined. 'This here girl can tell you all about the *murder* last night. Her name's Tina Dobbs, as you all know, an' this is her mother. Her mother, Missus Dobbs, takes in washin'. I took some clothes over to be washed this mawnin', and I found her an' her fambly in a right convulsive condition. At fust they was afraid an' ashamed to speak up, but I finally dragged the truth outa them. Tina can tell you all about the murder.'

Cole, as well as the others in the room, looked at the forlorn girl. Ash wondered what was coming next.

'All right, child, what have you got to tell us?' Cole asked.

'She ain't no child, Judge; she's full growed at sixteen,' the mother spoke up.

'All right, all right,' Cole said impatiently. 'A man's life is at stake here; let's not quibble. Speak up, Tina.'

The girl, her eyes downcast, began in a hesitant voice. 'I delivered some clothes Missus Haskell needed right bad for a birthday party today. Ma didn't get them ironed till late. I knew there was men drinkin' and prowlin' the town, so I took the back road to Haskell's. Coming back, I took a short cut across the empty lot above the hardware store. The moon was half full, givin' enough light to see by. A man, who must have been watching me, jumped up from a ditch and grabbed me. He started pawing me and tried to kiss me. I fought him back. He tore my dress half off, and I was scared plumb outa my mind. He had a gun stuck in the belt of his pants. I managed to grab the gun, and I shot without aiming. He dropped like a clubbed bull. I threw the gun into the ditch and run home. I was ashamed to tell what happened.'

'I made her tell me, Judge, but she was stubborn about facin' strangers. Blacky Brown convinced her she had to tell to save a man's life. He made her put on this torn dress as evidence of what happened.'

Cole looked around and scowled. 'Bein' as there was only one man killed last night, and in light of the testimony this girl was brave enough to give, I declare Stenner's death justifiable homicide and turn Mister Ashford Larkin free to pursue his business.'

'Just a minute!' Lundy protested. 'Bigge took our guns away! Stenner was an ornery cuss when drunk. He might have attacked this girl, but he was unarmed.'

Jeff Alfora spoke up against Lundy. 'You know as well as I do, Mitch, Stenner always carried an extra gun in his warbag; a gun with four notches on it.'

Blacky Brown reached under his coat and drew forth a gun which he held up for all to see. The four notches on the butt were plainly visible. 'You mean this gun that I picked up outa the ditch where the gal throwed it?'

There was a moment of tense silence, and then a guttural surge of sound went across the room. Sentiment was totally against the Big men. Lundy and his crew left the room in a body for their own protection, not trusting the temper of the townsmen. They were still unarmed. The women threw stones at them when they reached the street, and a free-for-all battle began. Lundy and his men fought off the attack as they worked their way toward the Last Chance. Ash Larkin watched the melee with satisfaction from the sidelines. When they reached the Last Chance, they backed in and closed the heavy door behind them.

Larkin, now more or less the hero of the moment, went to the back door of the saloon, which led to Leffa's living quarters. He knocked on the door, and Michele opened it. She pulled him in and closed and latched the door behind him.

'Thank God Lundy and his crew didn't have their way, Ash. They were bound to see you dead, just because I was nice to you.'

'It wasn't that, Mike. They had another reason.'

'Because you wouldn't leave the bar when they told you to?'

'It's deeper than that.' He explained about his disaster on the drive to Denver and how he suspected the Big men had caused it. 'They're afraid of me, Mike, afraid I might prove them guilty.'

'But you have no proof, have you?'

'Only their guilty consciences. Let's go into the bar; I don't want them to think I'm dodging them. Is Bigge there?'

'Bigge's there, and proddy as a bull. You see, we girls shoved him through the trap door into the beer cellar and locked him in. We didn't want him throwing his weight around at the trial.'

'I'll be doggoned!'

Ash led the way into the bar, not wishing to appear to be hiding behind a woman. The Big men turned ugly, sullen faces toward him. Bigge was pacing the floor, his beefy shoulders hunched and his square face a mask of stone. As Ash appeared, Boris stopped his pacing and glowered at him.

'You ain't been nothing but bad luck to me, boy. You got the whole town riled up ag'in' me an' my men. Nothing like this has happened before.'

'Yore men brung it on themselves, Bigge. They're guilty men, tryin' to bury their guilt by euchrin' me. I ain't about to die. I aim to go back to my ranch an' prosper,' Ash said defiantly.

'Look here, younker,' Bigge said, his big hands flexing to control his anger, 'I reckon you'll prosper a mite faster some place else; say Zion, in Utah. The Mormons might take you in. Or you could hang around Fort

Bridger and sign on with a wagon train for Californy. Here's two hundred dollars—' Bigge slapped the banknotes on the bar—'to pay for yore sorry spread. Hear me good. Never set foot in Jackson Hole or try to run cattle on the Puma Range. This money will give you a start away from me; I never want to see or hear of you again!'

Strange thoughts invaded and converged in Larkin's mind. He went quietly to the bar, picked up his money, gave Michele a kiss to spite Lundy and left the bar without a word. Bigge watched him go, a shadow in his ice-blue eyes. Quiet men made him uneasy.

CHAPTER FIVE

Ash Larkin sat in the office of the headquarters camp of the Thorson Sheep Company near the new settlement of Idaho Falls on the Snake River. It was a room of benches and stumps for chairs and plank-topped tables for desks. It was connected to the commissary, a big log structure roofed with a mud and straw thatch. There was a man doing accounts at one of the tables, and he sent an Indian boy helper to fetch Mister Thorson. When Thorson came in through the door to the commissary, Larkin rose, fumbling with his beaver sombrero.

'Sit down, Larkin. We don't stand on ceremony here,' Thorson told him.

Ash was puzzled at the appearance of the man before him. Thorson wasn't a tall man, but he gave the impression of being tall. He had iron-gray hair, and a face that had been lined by the vicissitudes of life. He gave little impression of aggressiveness, but one sensed an unyielding core under his placid exterior. He could have passed for a schoolteacher or a minister until one considered he had built a sheep empire against the opposition and aggression of the cattlemen. Ash sat down laying his hat on the floor. 'I hope I ain't interferin' with yore business, Mister Thorson,' Ash apologized, giving the older man the respect his appearance required.

'What can I do for you?' Jim Thorson inquired.

'Maybe I can do something for you. Do you know a man by the name of Blacky Brown who lives over the Wyoming border in a settlement called Wolf Bait?'

'That old rascal? What devilment is he up to now?'

'I reckon he ain't up to no devilment hisself, but he suggested I take a trail that could lead me plumb through Purgatory with a chance to end up in Hades,' Larkin explained solemnly.

'I don't follow you, Larkin.'

'Did you offer Brown a job breakin' into some new range near Jackson Hole?'

'We talked about it. It would be a chancey business. Blacky was too involved with some outlandish scheme he had at the time.' Thorson shrugged.

'Suppose I offered to take that chance, Mister Thorson?' Ash said calmly, brushing back his shaggy brown hair. 'What would you say to that, sir?'

Thorson took his time answering while he fiddled with a pencil on the table. His shrewd brown eyes evaluated the man before him.

'I'd say you were either a man on loco weed or a man with a grudge.'

'Make it a grudge,' Larkin told him.

'It must be a big grudge.'

'Big enough.'

'Tell it,' Thorson said cryptically.

Larkin narrated his misfortunes in detail, ending up with the commotion in Wolf Bait. He explained Boris Bigge's threats if he should ever ride into the Hole, and the pin money Boris had paid him for his ranch and his range.

'I ain't particular grieved about losin' my ranch and range; they can be recreated elsewhere. But the killin' of my pardner—a pardner who looked to me for advice and protection—can only be exonerated through blood and redemption.'

'I'm not sure you'd be a good risk, Larkin;

you're boiling too hard inside.'

'You goin' to find a man to take the risk without a cause besides money?'

'I don't know. I need a strong but cautious man. There's apt to be bloodshed and maybe killing,' Thorson warned.

'A man has to die some day; better to die for a reason than to shuck off from pure debility. As far as I'm concerned, there's already been a killin'—my buddy. My only drawback is I ain't never been within smellin' distance of a herd of sheep.'

'They have their own smell, like every other herd—human, animal, or fowl. Reckon sometimes the camp tender smells worse than the sheep. But that's beside the point. I'll furnish a Basque shepherd, one of the best, and his boy to tend camp. Manuel Elmora is a good man with the courage of a badger. His boy's name is Juan, John to you,' Thorson explained.

'You talk like I got the job, Mister Thorson.'

'Call me Jim. This may be a short acquaintance. You'll be the scout for the herd, Larkin.'

'Call me Ash. If me an' Elmora, with a runty kid to side us, are goin' to challenge the Hole, it will be a danged short acquaintance,' Larkin countered.

'Oh, I'll rustle up a stand-by crew you can

call on if things get rough,' Thorson assured him.

'Suppose I lose the herd?'

'I'll send you another herd. I've got sheep from the Bitterroots all the way down the Uintas. I've busted ranges before. Cowmen say cattle won't graze where sheep have browsed. That's pure ignorance. If sheep are permitted to crowd up too much, they trample out more feed than they eat. Cattle won't graze after them 'cause they don't leave anything for the cattle to eat. My Basques have orders to run a loose herd. There's range adjacent to cattle range that's good for nothing but sheep. Sheep can get by on black sage, rabbit brush, or juniper needles. In the winter they exist on the shadscale flats, eating snow for water. Cold doesn't get to them, not with three or four inches of wool on their backs—especially the merino with its tight fleece.'

'I reckon I've been told all that before, Thor—Jim, but I still ain't sure I can tell the dogs from the sheep.' Ash grinned.

'The dogs will introduce themselves, Ash. I've got mostly collies with some St. Bernard in them to give them body enough to stand off the timber wolves and coyotes. I imported a few shelties from England, smaller than collies but smart and fast. They're bred in the Shetland Islands off Scotland.'

'Sounds like you're in the sheep business real proper like. I've seen woolie owners who ain't much of a cut above buffalo hunters,' Ash mused.

'Organization and honesty pay off, Ash. How are you going about this range busting, and what do you expect out of the caper if it pays off?'

'I been thinkin' on both counts. First off, the bustin'. I aim to make a play for part of Jackson Hole. There must be benchland near the foot of the Tetons too grizzly for cattle.'

'The Hole is the benchland, son. The Tetons rise right up out of the ground like the fingers of God, two thirds of their carcasses above timberline. Even a mountain goat couldn't claw his way up some of them pinnacles.'

'There's possibilities farther north, towards Colter's Hell where them water spouts shoot up outa the ground, or eat over the Togwotee Pass. Fact is, I aim to get my Puma Valley Range back.'

'And you'd use sheep to do that?'

'Amen. Now for yore second question, about my remuneration: I want to get another start on a herd of cattle, Jim. You say you got sheep scattered from the Bitterroots to the Uintas. All right; you stake me to the first herd of sheep I make stick around the Hole.'

Thorson's lean face assumed a querulous expression, and his brown eyes half closed. 'I thought you aimed to go into the *cattle* business, Ash, not the despised sheep business. What's the connection?'

'There will be a connection. I aim to take the money I get from the sheep and buy cattle. It won't cost you nothin', Jim. I'll pay for the sheep little by little once I git 'stablished.'

'That's not the point, lad. I'll be out other money. I'll have to hire three gunslicks to back you up in case the cowmen declare war. It isn't easy to buy men to fight for a *sheep* outfit. They've got to be men with guts and grudges. They don't come cheap. If I go to all this trouble and then you sell off the sheep, I'll be right back where I started from. I'm backing the caper, if I do back it, to open up new range and keep it opened up.'

'I didn't say I'd sell off the herd. I said I'll take the money the herd brings in to buy cattle. The time is here in Wyoming when cattlemen will realize that a one-crop range is a chancey business. A lot of cow outfits have been ruined by a hard Wyoming winter. They come periodically. Sheep have a fifty percent better chance of pullin' through the worst winter I've seen. The fact is, I aim to run cattle and sheep.'

'On the same range?' Thorson inquired, deeply interested in Larkin's proposition.

'No. There's range fit for sheep that cattle won't prosper on. If I make a go of it, the cattlemen might wise up and diversify the range. Sheep or cattle ain't the object of the hard, chancey ranch business; it's money in the pocket that counts,' Ash said seriously.

'Larkin, I like your cut; you're thinking my way. It's too late in the year to invade the Hole this winter, but I'll tell you what we'll do. I'll give you a letter to Fernando Lopez, the foreman of my Uinta ranch. He'll fix you up with a herd an' outfit, and he'll send Manuel Elmora and his kid along to herd the sheep. Don't head straight for the Hole. Go north by way of Rock Springs and stay east of the Divide. You can winter the herd on the shadscale flats along the Wind River. The ewes will drop their lambs in May. By June when the Togwotee Pass is open—it's ten thousand feet high—the lambs will be strong enough to travel. That's when you make your play for the Hole.'

Ash pondered this. His revenge on Bigge wasn't going to be simple. It meant at least eight months on the trail through strange territory with a herd of sheep, which were anathema in some quarters. By the time he reached the Hole, revenge could be ashes in his mouth. He turned the thing over in his mind and looked at the other side. By next summer Bigge and the other ranchers in the Hole would not be expecting him; he could catch them with their guard down.

Thorson, noticing his hesitation, inquired, 'Sound too tough for you, Ash? I might find other men to break that range, but you've got the best excuse. Your Puma range is not far from the Pass.'

'I was just ponderin' the obstacles, Jim. What about the men with guts an' grudges?'

'You won't need them until you cross the Togwotee. I can't afford to pay fighting wages to men to have them lay about all winter. Besides, it takes time to find men willing to risk their skins for sheep. Even if they win the war, they'll be branded "Stinkos" from then on. I'll send a scout to find your men. There's a lot of renegades running loose in the Indian Territory along the Arkansas, some of them with mean grudges against society in general.'

'You sure them renegades, as you call 'em, won't turn on me?' Ash queried, half in jest.

'My scout will pick up the right men. They'll be waiting for you in Dubois near the Togwotee in May.'

When Ash left Idaho Falls, he didn't follow the Snake River, but headed northeast toward Teton Pass. His pride wouldn't let him run away from Boris Bigge without some show of defiance. He had expected a swifter revenge, but perhaps a lingering worry would niggle Bigge like a bur under the blanket. He had gone from Leffa's place without a word of defiance, taking Bigge's money with him. He had taken the money not so much because he had needed it, but to confuse the man who believed he had bought him for so cheap a price. Now, with the expense money Thorson had advanced him, he would return the money he had silently picked up from Leffa's bar. There were some things Bigge couldn't buy.

Larkin rode into the settlement, which could hardly be called a town. The log buildings were grouped haphazardly around the trading post that dominated them. Dismounting before the trading post, Larkin entered the dim interior. The smell of raw hides, dried meat, sowbelly, and oiled leather nauseated him for a moment, but it was a smell a man soon got used to. It took time for his eyes to adjust to the niggardly light that came in through the slit windows. It was a typical trading post, with bags of beans and flour stacked in the middle of the floor. From nails and rafter hooks hung pots and pans, boots, bridles and snowshoes. On one side there was a counter behind which shelves were stocked with various kinds of merchandise. Not until his eyes were accustomed to the dim light did he see the girl behind the counter.

'What can I do for you, mister?' she inquired.

Larkin bellied up to the counter and scrutinized her. She was far from Indian, with light brown hair and hazel eyes. Her oval face was soft and smooth, and in the semi-darkness she appeared to be as tanned as a cowboy. The hands on the counter were slim, with long fingers.

'Well?' she prompted, fidgeting under his scrutiny.

'Pardon, miss. Yore presence here was a mite unexpected. I didn't know they raised American beauties here in the Hole,' Ash said ardently.

'If that's a compliment, keep it. I doubt if you've ever seen a real beautiful woman,' she replied. 'Did you come here to talk, trade or travel?'

'A little bit of all three.'

'If you want a drink, go through that door at the back. My brother's tending bar there.'

'The drink can wait. My name's Larkin, Ash Larkin. I'm lookin' for Boris Bigge; I owe him some money,' Ash said.

'Everybody owes him money, Mister Larkin. That's the way he likes it. Keeping folks in debt gives him a harness on them—a lever. To an honest man an obligation is a hobble he can't shake off, so the creditor manages him with the threat of bankruptcy.'

'That's why I want to pay him off,' Ash told her. 'He threw his weight around in Wolf Bait and backed hisself into a corner. He figgered to buy me off.'

The girl leaned closer and studied him. 'You're not the man who turned the tables on the Big brand in Wolf Bait, are you?'

'I don't know about turning tables. He

pushed me an' I pushed back, with a little help from my friends.'

The girl laughed outright, a lilting, pleasant sound.

'Let me in on the joke,' Ash suggested.

'Boris is still steamed up about that stalemate in Wolf Bait. On top of that, Leffa Hanks turned him down again.'

'What's with him and Leffa? I figger she's a fool or a hard bargainer, to turn him down. Why does he hanker after her in particular?'

'No one has ever explained why a man hankers after a woman—one woman. A fool allows that all women are alike, the same as cattle. A wise man ascribes it to the alchemy of nature, which, after all, manages ninety-eight percent of our lives awake or sleeping. Nature is always selective, striving for improvement. There must be something in Leffa that something in Boris needs, some deeper concern than he understands himself.'

Ash let out a slow whistle. 'Did you pick up all that wisdom here in the Hole?'

'Books can be acquired anywhere. Schiller, Nietzsche and Schopenhauer are there for everyone to read.'

'Look, sister, I don't know what you're doing here in this God-forsaken place readin' all them philosophers. You belong out in the world. You got beauty an' brains; why waste them here?'

'My father owns this trading post. I like it

here. I prefer to think that God hasn't forsaken Jackson's Hole as much as he has the big cities. Sodom and Gomorrah thrived and perished of their own evil, but even then this spot of beauty flourished. Men invented evil, and they take it with them wherever they go.'

'A preacher, too. You're a female of many talents. What's yore name?' Ash inquired belatedly.

'Heather.'

'Nice name. With a beauty like you around, I don't see why Boris looks outside the Hole.'

'I'm one of the little Bigges; Boris is my father.'

That stopped Ash for a moment. 'And yore mother?'

'She was killed by a bear.'

'I'm sorry to hear that, Heather.'

'My mother was a woman of refinement. Boris brought her out here from Saint Louis, Missouri. She got in some sort of trouble there, and Boris helped her out. I was never told what the trouble was, but she came West with him and never went back. Robin and I were born here in Beaver Dam. My mother taught us to read and cipher, and she had brought a lot of books with her which we were encouraged to study.'

'Didn't she explain to you about the outside world? Didn't she want you to get out of the Hole?' Ash inquired, perplexed.

'She told us about the outside world, Ash Larkin. She told us that out there people lie and cheat and destroy each other for money. She said that honesty and integrity is an illusion men wear like their shirts. When it is soiled, they put on a new one, but they let nothing stand in the way of getting the advantage, of making a profit, or of ruining another in order to acquire his worldly goods. She was a bitter woman who had looked under the rug where the orts of greed and deception were swept out of sight.'

Ash was shaken by the girl's intensity. 'Now wait just a minute, Heather Bigge. Some of what yore mother said is true, but there's two sides to every coin. Some men do all the things your mother said, and some of them grow rich and famous by doin' 'em. There's more rascals high up in the government than you'll find in a rustlers' hideout. On the other hand, most ordinary folks scrabble honest for a livin', raise their kids in the fear of God and die peaceable. Reckon I never did figger why you had to *fear* God, but that's what they tell us.'

'I don't fear God, Ash Larkin.'

'But you're afeared of life. Just tell me where I can find yore pa. I didn't see no house in the settlement big enough to fit a man with his talents,' Ash said.

'We don't live in the settlement. Did you

see that tree-covered island just off shore?'

'I reckon I didn't give it much thought.'

'That's where we live.'

'How do you git across the water?'

'There's a ferry. We pull our way over on a rope.'

'Is that where yore mother got killed by the bear?'

'No. We lived on the Snake then. Pa took my mother's death real hard. He moved to the island and exterminated the animals.'

'I reckon animals can swim,' Ash reminded her.

'Pa has a rider who does nothing but look for invaders. It's mostly for my protection. He has a crazy fear that I might be attacked like my mother was.'

'How about here, in the settlement, Heather? You could be attacked here, even in the store, if the door was left open.'

She reached under the counter and brought out one of the latest repeating rifles, levered it expertly and put it to her shoulder. 'I can hit a knothole in a pine plank at a hundred yards, Larkin. Want a demonstration?'

'No. All I want is Mister Bigge.'

The unmistakable voice of Boris Bigge bellowed behind him from the direction of the bar. 'What the devil are you doing here, Larkin!'

CHAPTER SIX

Ash was unarmed. He had deliberately left his gun in his saddle bags for the simple reason that he wanted no gunplay to interfere with his long range plan.

'Reckon I come to see you, Bigge,' Ash said casually.

'Didn't I give you orders not to show your face in the Hole?' Bigge growled.

'Orders is a two-way trail—give an' take. I didn't take 'em.'

'You took my money.'

'As a loan, Mister Bigge, for which I'm under obligation. I've come to pay the money back.'

'That was no loan. It was full price for the sticks and stones you called a ranch,' Bigge said, curbing his temper.

'You've got no paper signed by me givin' up my ranch. I reckon it was a misunderstandin'. I aim to keep my ranch and prosper on it.'

'What do you aim to prosper with—jack rabbits and coyotes? What gives you the crazy notion that you're going to neighbor my range without molestation?'

'The neighborin' is my affair, Mister Bigge; the molestation is up to you. Have you ever seen a starling pick the eyes out of a hawk in full flight?'

'Have you got the gall to threaten *me*?' Bigge barked.

'Nope. Just quotin' parables. I opened up the Puma range, banked up the waterholes an' cleaned out the springs. I made peace with the Shoshones and even burned off the loco weed. I reckoned to manage that range, not exploit it. Things were comin' along real good until I got euchred. If for no other reason than to honor my murdered pardner, I aim to keep on managing that range.'

'You must've ate some of that loco weed you burned, Larkin. You can manage that range from hell to breakfast, but it won't make you no money unless you've got stock on it.'

'I aim to put stock on it.'

Bigge's ice-blue eyes narrowed. 'You hinted in Wolf Bait that the Big brand might be the cause of your troubles. If you got some crazy notion to whittle a profit out of my hide, remember this: rustlers hang high and die young. There's another place in the world for you, Larkin. There ain't no way you can build up another herd of cattle without my forbearance.'

'Mebbe I'll raise turkeys, Bigge.'

'Don't fun me, boy. There ain't no kind of livestock that can make money in Wyoming, 'cept cattle or sheep.' Bigge gave Ash a long look. 'You ain't in any remote way figuring on sheep?'

'You said it, Mister Bigge, not me. You're puttin' ideas in my head,' Ash said with a mirthless smile.

Heather, who had been listening to the exchange of words, spoke up. 'What's the matter, Pa? Are you getting scared? How can a lone cowboy with nothing on his hands but time disturb you so much that you want him out of the country?'

'I was a lone cowboy once,' Bigge mused. 'I fought for everything I've got and lost a good woman in the process. I don't figger to have another lone cowboy take it away from me.'

'I ain't hankerin' to take nothin' from you, Bigge. In the end, you might be glad I stuck around. In the meantime, I aim to have my ranch and my freedom. Here's yore two hundred dollars.' Ash put ten double eagles on the counter. The gold coins glowed in the subdued light.

'Pick it up, boy, and slope on out of here. What I said in Wolf Bait still goes: stay out of my way!'

'That gold ain't mine; it's yourn, Mister Bigge. As for gettin' out, I'll get out in my own time—and I'll come back in my own time. Right now I want to buy some grub.'

'Don't sell him anything, Heather,' Bigge ordered.

In direct defiance of her father, Heather asked, 'What do you need, Ash?'

Ash hesitated. 'I reckon I can live off the land for a spell, Heather. I ain't aimin' to get you into trouble. I figgered I'd stay in Beaver Dam for the night.'

'You've got an ornery streak in you, boy. I reckon that beating you took in Wolf Bait didn't temper it none.' Bigge turned to the saloon door. 'Robin, come in here!' he called.

A boy of about eighteen came into the store. He had a square face like his father, but his light brown hair and hazel eyes matched those of his sister. He wore a business-like gun tied low against his leg.

'What's up, Pa?' Robin asked.

'Go fetch Mitch Lundy; he's breaking broncs in the north corral. This younker here needs a refreshing of his memory.'

'Whipping a stubborn mule, Pa, won't make him budge; it makes him more stubborn,' Heather said.

'Then I'll build a fire under him. If he gets his belly hairs scorched, he'll listen to reason. Go fetch Lundy, Robin.'

'Aren't you big enough to take him yourself, Pa?' There was a jeer in Heather's voice.

'I can take him, Pa,' Robin declared, assuming the classic pose of a gunman about to declare himself.

'Take it easy, Robbie; he's unarmed,' Bigge cautioned.

'Then throw him a gun,' Robin ordered.

Heather reached under the counter and took out the rifle, laying it before her. 'If there's any shooting in here, I'll kill the man who lives,' she said quietly.

'Are you crazy, sis? This ranny was born to die. Might as well kill him before he takes a lot of other men with him,' Robin declared.

'Why don't you get him outside and back-shoot him?' Heather snapped.

'Shut up, both of you!' Bigge raised his voice. He stepped to the rack of guns, and with one motion his ham-like hand snatched a gun and tossed it toward Ash. Ash couldn't believe what was happening; he was being set up like a pig on the killing floor.

There was not time to think. The throw was high, and Ash lunged toward Robin, raising his hand to catch the forty-five and brought it down across Robin's wrist. Robin's gun exploded just as the heavy revolver struck his wrist with a crunching sound. Ash felt a club strike his left arm just before Robin's gun hit the floor.

Robin let out a yowl of rage and pain. 'He's busted my gun hand! Kill him, Pa, kill him!'

'Shut up!' Bigge growled. 'Maybe he done you a favor, boy. You're still alive. Now maybe you'll stop playing at being a gun-hawk. He saved some other ranny from boring your guts.'

Heather came from behind the counter with a rustle of skirts and a concerned look on her beautiful face.

'You've been hit, Ash. Let me see your arm,' she said, unbuttoning his shirt cuff and rolling up the sleeve.

'What do you call this, Bigge, the execution chamber?' Larkin inquired bitterly.

'I wanted to teach the kid a lesson. I figured you could take him. It's hell to be young *and* foolish, Larkin.'

'Or old and bitter,' Heather retorted. 'I'm afraid it smashed the bone, Ash. I'll have to take you to the island, where Washita, our Shoshone cook, can splint it properly.'

'What about me?' Robin said, a sob in his voice and tears in his eyes as he held up his smashed wrist.

'What about you, stupid?' Heather jeered. 'Come along. Washita is an expert at bone-setting.'

They crossed the narrow channel of water on the ferry in silence except for Robin's one threat. 'You've twisted my life, Larkin. I'm not forgetting that. One day you'll die for it!'

Larkin didn't bother to answer. The house in the clearing was a reflection of Boris Bigge. It was big. The lime-chinked logs of the two-story structure were whitewashed, and the roof was of hand-hewn shakes. The sun gleamed on the glass windows, and the flagstoned veranda had a high roof supported by tall pine poles, giving it a colonial appearance. The interior projected the character of a genteel woman, used to fine things. In the big open-hearth kitchen which boasted a cast iron cooking stove, Washita looked up from the batch of dough she was kneading, her dark hands white with flour.

'How you want now, Missy Heather? More loco braves get busted up for fool fight?' she asked in her pidgin English.

'Yes, Washita, more dumb braves get busted up. You fix,' Heather parroted her talk.

The smell of the new baked bread taken from the oven did nothing to alleviate the fiery pain in Larkin's arm, but it did a gnawing attack on his stomach. He submitted to the Indian woman's ministrations, gritting his teeth against the pain.

'Him no bad busted. Little bone bent; big bone him chip off.'

Heather was searching in the storeroom for slats and came back with some thin boards. Washita took a knife, scored the boards and snapped them off to the proper length. Ash looked ruefully at his bandaged arm, for which Heather fashioned a sling from a dish towel. Robin stepped forward, his face a grim mask of hate.

'How come a stranger gets proper treatment before me?' he demanded.

'Guests are served before members of the family,' Heather quipped.

'Don't get a yen for this cowboy, sis.

Reckon he won't last to sire any kids.'

'Robin, keep on like you're going, and you won't live to see him die,' Heather warned her brother.

'Reckon I'd better traipse on,' Ash said.

'You'll do nothing of the kind. You can't ride out of here with that bloody shirt. Washita, fetch this cowboy a clean shirt.'

'Not none of my shirts, Washy,' Robin warned.

'Your shirts wouldn't fit a *man*, Robin,' Heather said.

It was useless to object; he needed a clean shirt.

'You can't leave today, Ash,' Heather said. 'You've got to stay here overnight.'

The pain of his arm convinced him she was right.

The shirt came, and Heather insisted in helping him change. When he objected, she threatened to give him a bath. 'You could use one, Larkin,' she quipped.

'There's plenty of God's clean water out in the lake. I'll do my own bathing at a time I deem proper,' Ash informed her.

Washita took his shirt away to mend and wash. He felt lost in Boris' flannel shirt, two sizes too large for him. Heather rolled the sleeves up, but he tucked the shirt in his Levis himself. While they waited for dinner, Heather played on the pianoforte, beautiful music that touched Ash and made him marvel at the beautiful, complex girl seated at the instrument. In a way, Heather Bigge was being either selfish or cowardly in denying the world her beauty and talent.

'That was beautiful, Heather,' Ash applauded quietly.

'Mozart,' she explained. 'He was one of the first to compose for the pianoforte. My mother taught me to play.'

'Your mother must have been a most remarkable woman.'

'I told you that.'

'She did you a disservice, I reckon, with her caustic appraisal of the outside world. Talent like yours is made to be shared,' Ash admonished her gently.

'And your talents? What are you going to do with them? Fight and fuss and brawl until a bullet cuts you down? About the only real talent a cowboy has is an untouchable pride to cover up his ignorance,' she charged.

In a way she was right. The future he had embarked upon promised little more than privation, fighting, with a grim resolution to make his tipped-over world right again. His thoughts were cut off as Boris Bigge and another man came into the darkening room.

'That's the ranny I was telling you about, who made free with my daughter,' Boris said to the stranger without preliminaries.

Ash took umbrage at the remark. 'That's a loose statement, Mister Bigge. I ain't makin' free with nobody.'

'I share his resentment, Pa. I'm just being civil to a guest as my mother taught me,' Heather admonished.

'You're like your mother, dragging in strays, be they birds, beasts or bums. Your mother was too soft for this country, but she had a hardness in her you wouldn't understand.'

The last remark was made with a tinge of bitterness that puzzled Larkin. Before he could ponder on it, Bigge introduced the newcomer.

'Marty Blue, meet this pilgrim who's doggin' me like a hungry coyote. He calls himself Ash Larkin. I ain't sure what he's hungry for; some kind of revenge, I think. At least that's sticking in his craw. He was formerly from Puma Valley. He's got a notion I wronged him.'

Marty Blue was a smaller man in stature than Bigge, but he was hard and bulky-looking. He had a nose like a potato stuck between his deep eyes. Ash nodded to him, but he looked at Boris.

'You got yore facts a mite twisted, Mister Bigge,' Larkin said calmly, 'I'm still from Puma Valley across the Winds, and a notion, if it's nurtured hard enough, can become a flamin' sword.'

Marty Blue scratched his potato nose. 'He's a right smart talker, Boris, but ain't you scarin' up one of them chimeras? He ain't got a goat's body nor a lion's haid, and he ain't breathin' no fire, only a little harmless smoke. A lad without some spunk ain't wuth his salt. What can he do to us?'

'He's stubborn and grudgy. He ain't comfortable to have around.'

'You ought to know about stubbornness, Bigge,' Ash interposed. 'How come you men came to top-dog the Hole if you wasn't stubborn?'

'You can make yourself a heap of trouble for no purpose, or you can ride away from it,' Bigge advised.

'You almost had me killed today, Bigge,' Ash said grimly, indicating his slinged arm.

'Bull dust!' Bigge snorted. 'I figured Robin needed a lesson. You taught him.'

'I spilled blood in the teachin'. I ain't forgettin' that.'

'Simmer down,' Blue said. 'Save the bickerin' for the bunkhouse or the barn. There's a mighty pretty lady present.'

In the ensuing conversation, Larkin learned that Blue held the range to the north, part of it in Colter's Hell, that area of yellowstones with water spouts spurting toward the sky. There was another top-dog in the hole, Mose Kindle. They were called in to supper, and the talk turned to a discussion of the coming winter, the amount of hay they had stacked and the price Bigge had gotten for the beef at the railroad. As soon as they had eaten, Ash excused himself.

CHAPTER SEVEN

Ash didn't go to the bunkhouse; he walked through the moonlight to the ferry and pulled himself across with his good arm. Reaching the mainland, he headed up the bluff to the trading post, hoping to get his horse and rig without running into any of the Big brand hands. He wanted no more petty quarrels. His next run-in with the Big brand would be make or break. The front of the trading post was dark, but the back room which contained the bar was illuminated by a couple of bleary lanterns. He flung open the door and stepped into the room, which was fetid with the odor of unwashed men, spilled whiskey and trap bait. Two hairy men with beaver caps were playing cards at the only table. Their bearskin coats were draped over the benches on which they sat. There was no one else in the room but the mestizo or half-breed barkeep.

'What for you come here to have, *señor*?' the barkeep asked.

'I am Ash Larkin. I got this in the trading post this afternoon.' Ash indicated his bandaged arm.

'I have hear of this, *señor*. Why for you no

stay at the Casa Grande weeth the *señorita*?'

'For reasons of my own, hombre. I want my horse and gear. Where is it?'

'In the stable behind this cantina.'

'*Gracias*. Can you sell stuff from the store?'

'*Si*, why not? What do you weesh?'

'I want to buy a shirt. This one belongs to Boris Bigge; I wouldn't deprive him of it,' Larkin said grimly.

'We have only three sizes, *señor*: leetle, meedle, and beeg. Also is only two color, black and not so black,' the barkeep explained gravely.

'Get me one of the middle size, black,' Ash ordered, taking off Bigge's shirt and laying it on the bar. The mestizo returned with a flannel shirt which fitted over the bandage and splints a little snugly. He also had some advice.

'You had better ride *muy pronto*, *señor*. The men from the bunkhouse weel be coming up for their *bora la noche*, their nightcap. They have no affection for you.'

Ash laid two dollars on the bar. 'A dollar for the shirt and a dollar for the stable, *amigo*.'

The barkeep poured a slug of whiskey. 'One on the *casa*, *señor* You look like a troubled man. There is a lantern in the barn, and here ees a *forsforo* to light it weeth.' He proffered Ash a block of matches.

'I'm obliged, *amigo*.'

Downing the slug, Larkin took the matches and went out into the moonlight. The stable was close behind the cantina, as the mestizo had said. His horse was contentedly munching wild hay. Ash didn't strike a match; there was enough moonlight for him to find his rig and cinch it on his horse. The flare of a match would be a signal to prowlers of his whereabouts. Lundy and his crew would have heard of the shooting in the store and his subsequent trip to the island with Heather. They would believe he was still there, which suited Larkin just fine. He mounted and rode quietly from the shadow of the stable, keeping off the main paths of the village. As he skirted a clump of cottonwoods, he saw figures walking from the direction of the Big brand bunkhouse. He wondered if the barkeep would hold his tongue. There were the two trappers to contend with, but trappers and cowboys seldom fraternized.

He headed for the spine of the Wind River range, keeping off the trails until the moon went down and he neared Togwotee Pass.

He didn't ride directly to his cabin; he stopped in a high bunch of chaparral and watched to see if anybody, presuming him dead, had squatted on the place. At first he saw no signs of life, and then the figure of a familiar burro, browsing at the stream, caught his eye. He grinned and rode on confidently. Where Napoleon, the burro appeared, could Yancy Kobeck be far behind? Smoke was curling from the chimney, and Ash anticipated a welcome he had not even dreamed of. His nose sniffed the smell of boiling coffee, and his mouth watered for the sourdough biscuits and molasses which were Yancy's favorites.

As he rode into the yard, Yancy greeted him from the doorway with a rifle over his arm. Larkin rode into the lane, which was carpeted with golden leaves from the cottonwood trees, and almost past the log barn, which was fifty yards from the house, before recognition dawned on the oldster. Yancy discarded the rifle and raised his arms, waggling his hands as a sign of recognition. As Ash dismounted near the front stoop, Yancy was there to grab his hand.

'You old catamount—' Ash grinned—'I thought you was goin' to put a hole through my gizzard!'

'My eyes ain't what they used to be, son. Reckon I figgered I was seein' a ghosty. I heered a rumor you was daid. Where's Virg? Ain't he with you?'

'No, he ain't. I'll tell you about it after I get this hoss watered, rubbed down an' stabled,' Larkin said gravely.

The old man ran a gnarled hand through his straggly gray hair, then down his tobacco-stained whiskers. 'He ain't the one who' daid, is he?'

'I told you I'll explain. You git inside an' pour out the sourdough. Make plenty of them buscuits,' Larkin told him.

His horse taken care of, Larkin bone-weary from the long ride, went into the neat cabin.

'Yancy, you old coot, you don't know how glad I am to see you here. I figured on a cold camp.'

'When I heard the rumor you was ambushed, Ash boy, I said to myself, "Yanc, you might as well winter in Ash's cabin. Hit'll be snug an' warm, an' in case the rumor ain't true, you can keep a eye on things for him." So here I be, dispossessed jest when I got the place housekept an' livable.'

'Wait a minute, old-timer; you ain't dispossessed yet. Get the hog meat fryin', an' I'll fill you in on what happened to me an' Virg.'

Larkin told Yancy about the stampede on the trail, the shooting, and how Virgil Culp was lost and probably ravaged by coyotes. He told about his experience in Wolf Bait, and about the confrontation with Bigge and his kids.

Yancy listened in glum silence, grunting a curse under his breath now and then. When Ash had finished, Yancy shook his bearded head.

'Boy, you got a problem you jest can't walk away from,' he opined.

'I know it, Yanc.'

'It's a problem that could kill you. You got no cattle, you got only pocket money, an' you got range hawks ready to swoop down on yore range. Not much to build on, Ash.'

'I got more than that, Yanc. I got me a big hate to soften, a revenge on the hyenas who stomped me out, an' a poison in my system that I got to get rid of. I'm dead sure it was the crew of the Big brand that brought me disaster. I aim to gut-shoot the man who killed Virg and cut Bigge down to proper size.'

'And how in God's world are you goin' to perform that miracle?' Yancy snorted. 'Yore left arm don't look so good.'

Ash didn't divulge anything about his partnership with Thorson. He wanted no hint of his sheep plans to get to the Hole. His answer to Yancy was, 'The Lord moves in mysterious ways his wonders to perform.'

'I reckon you'll need the Lord, a few of the saints, and a goodly army of the devil's best, or I should say *worst* men, to put contrition in the way of them top dogs in the Hole. They got where they are by bein' tough an' ignorin' the Holy Trinity. You goin' to spank 'em today or tomorra?'

'Make it tomorrow, Yanc. I'm goin' away. I'm not sure when I'll be back, but I'll be back. You stay here for the winter. I reckon yore trappin' an' prospectin' days are gettin' a mite troublesome, ain't they?'

'I ain't as spry as I once was. That don't make me no clinker.'

'You're not a clinker, Yanc; you still got fire in you. It's jest that I might need a man of yore ilk who knows this country like his own hand, once I commence the resurrection.'

'You talk like a Mormon proselyter, but you ain't convinced me of the miracle. Howsomever, when you come back I'll still be the defender of yore house an' hearth.'

CHAPTER EIGHT

At Blacky's cabin, Ash related all that had happened since their last meeting.

'So you really went an' done it—hitched up with Thorson. I almost done the same myself, but the range I aimed to break was in Injun territory. The Injuns welcomed the sheep; they was easier to steal than cattle. They could be milked; they had wool for blankets on 'em. You're pickin' the toughest range around, an' with a broke arm, too.'

'It happens to border on my range, Blacky. The arm will heal.'

As he headed for the Uintas, Blacky's warning rattled around in his head. He had picked the toughest range around, but if you could break the tough one, the others would be much easier. He avoided Fort Bridger on his way south, recalling the warm look in Mary Flynn's green Irish eyes when she looked at him. He wanted to cause no rift between Mary and Sergeant Flynn, her husband. They had befriended him, and though Mary had been an angel of mercy to him, jealousy was an emotion easily aroused in the West, where women, good women were few and far between.

He reached Thorson's Uinta camp as the first snow began to fall. The place was a confusion of activity as the outfits were being repaired and provisioned for the winter ahead on the shadscale flats to the north and east. There was a storehouse of logs and headquarter building of logs and mud. Word of Ash's coming and his future intentions had been sent south by Thorson with a trusted messenger. Fernando Lopez, manager of the camp, was expecting him.

Ash showed the paper Thorson had given him. 'Reckon you know more'n I do what I need for this caper, Lopez,' Ash said.

'*Seguro*. Manuel Elmora and his son Juan have a herd of four thousand head ready for the trail north. When you hit the range you're tryin' to break, *amigo*, commit only half the herd the first time so you'll have another herd for a second try.'

'And if that try don't work?'

'We'll send another herd for next spring.

Thorson has had to fight his way onto a lot of range, but it pays off, sometimes even for the cattlemen, if they have enough savvy to realize it.'

Ash met Elmora and his son Juan. The Basque was a short man, no taller than his young son. He had the placid, self-effacing manner of the sheep-herder who, living with solitude and the serenity of the stars, imbibes the peace and patience of nature. He spoke fair English. His son Juan was a smooth-skinned lad with wide, watchful eyes and straight black hair that hung below his battered hat like a shawl caressing his shoulders. Ash discovered a thoughtful wisdom in Manuel Elmora to which he listened with respect.

'There is no need for you to stay weeth the herd, *Señor* Larkin. Juan and myself can handle the herd very well across the open prairie country. We weel take the time. The winter browse ees very sparse. Sometimes the shadscale thorns pierce the ewes' lips and must be removed. Then the lambing weel slow down the herd in May. By that time we'll be close to Dubois. You can meet us there.'

The plan sounded feasible, but Ash looked at the slim figure of Juan and the stocky but erect figure of Manuel. 'Are you sure you two can wrangle that big herd, *señor*?' Ash inquired.

Manuel shook his head. 'Not me, *amigo*; the dogs. The dogs are the real shepherds, constantly alert, constantly ferreting out stray bunches of ewes, constantly on the lookout for danger from coyotes, wolves or lions. I have herded sheep all my life, *señor*.'

'And Juan, is that to be his life also?'

Manuel shrugged. *'Quien sabe?* Who knows? It is a life close to God and the earth. The wild animals we contend weeth keel only for food. We avoid the most vicious animal of all, man.'

Ash wanted to ask about his wife, but he didn't pry. 'I'll start out with you, Manuel, to see for sure you're on the way.'

The first few days on the trail Larkin became accustomed to the smell of sheep, to the constant blatting and the notes of the various bells swinging from the necks of the black markers. There were a percentage of black sheep among the white, and they were the ones counted to make a check on the herd. If the black sheep were all there, it was reasonable to believe the herd was intact. If a black sheep were missing, a search was made for it, and when found it had its percentage of white sheep with it. Ash marveled at the dogs, who were sometimes commanded by gestures from long distances. There appeared to be an understanding between the sheep and the dogs. When the dogs appeared, barking their commands, the sheep turned in a body and moved in the direction the dogs indicated.

Juan ran the camp, cooked the meals and slept inside the camp wagon. Manuel slept outside in spite of the cold, wrapped in his sheepskin coat and a buffalo robe. Ash had his own blanket roll in which he slept under the wagon, not presuming to request the sanctuary of the bed in the wagon. He trailed with the herd for a week until they were at the Green River east of Fort Bridger. There he left them, deciding to spend part of the winter at the fort in spite of the presence of Mary Flynn. He owed them a visit to let them know of his progress since they had nursed him from the brink of death. The rendezvous with the herd at Dubois in the spring suited him fine, as that was where he was to meet the hired gunfighters who were to help protect the herd. Before leaving the herd, he asked Manuel to help him remove the last of the bandage from his arm.

'Juan can do that for you, *señor*,' Manuel told him. 'Hees hands are not yet horny.'

Juan asked him into the neat camp wagon with its efficient arrangement: the stove beside the door, small but adequate, the table that was hinged on the side so it could be lifted out of the way. The seats on either side, under which were bins for supplies, were scrubbed, and the small cupboards with their gingham curtains contained dishes and cutlery anchored in such a way they could not fall out as the wagon lumbered over the rough terrain. The double bed across the rear of the wagon was covered by a buffalo robe.

'I reckon you can untie them cloth strings, *amigo*. It's a might awkward for a man with one free arm,' Ash said.

Juan, a self-effacing lad who spoke only when spoken to, nodded. He had the hands of an artist or a musician, and Ash visualized them growing gnarled and horny as the years went by. The job completed, Juan averted his eyes.

'*Vaya con Dios*, *señor*; go with God. You are *un bravo hombre*. Take the care your *coraje* is not too much for your strength.' That was a long speech for Juan, spoken in his faltering, changing voice.

'A man never knows the size of his courage, Juan, until he is called upon to use it. I'll see you in Dubois, *muchacho*.'

'I am not the *muchacho* any longer, *señor*, I am *un hombre*, a man.'

'*Si, hombre, perdonar*,' Ash apologized.

He reached Fort Bridger near dusk and found the walls of the fort surrounded by emigrant wagon trains resting up and taking on supplies for the rugged journey ahead. Some were electing to winter at the fort, fearful of the fate that had overtaken the Donner party in the high Sierras. Others decided to push on toward Salt Lake City, that the Mormons called Zion, and winter there. There were few trains compared to earlier in the year; these were the laggards who had been visited by misfortune or disease. Jim Bridger had built the trading post years before to cater to the westward migration of an expanding nation. The Mormons had forced him out, taking over the lucrative trade until the place had burned. Then it had been rebuilt by the army, who now controlled it.

Ash, who had become a well-known figure during his long convalescence at the fort, was welcomed with friendly greetings on all sides. He was even asked to have supper with Major Shorter and his wife Cynthia, but he refused politely, explaining he had a previous invitation from Sergeant Flynn and his wife Mary.

The sergeant and Mary greeted him warmly, Mary with such enthusiasm it made him uneasy. After eating, they chatted until Larkin insisted on finding a bed in the barracks. There he heard a man in a card game remark that he was headed toward the Indian Territory to recruit some men for Jim Thorson. When Ash got the man alone, he introduced himself.

'So you're the ranny who Thorson is recruitin' the gunswifts fer? Ain't nobody told you range breakin' fer sheep is a touchy business? Most herds don't make it.'

'That's all I've heard, mister. Thorson said it would take a man with guts and a grudge. I've got the grudge; the guts will have to prove themselves. This is a hush-hush business.'

'I been cautioned on that.'

'What's yore name?'

'Dixon.'

'How about if I go with you to pick out the men?'

'No way. If you was seen out there sizin' up gun-hawks, word would get back to Bigge, and he'd be waitin' for you. Better you should range the Hole, lettin' Bigge think you a loner.'

Ash was finally convinced of Dixon's wisdom. He remained at Bridger for a month, doing some hunting for the commissary and exercising his left arm to limber it up. He was a right-handed man, but sometimes his left came in handy. He practiced drawing and shooting on the rifle range, getting back some of his gun savvy. He circulated among the wagon trains, selling his skill at blacksmithing and harness repairing. He kept out of Mary Flynn's way as much as possible, but the day he decided to head north, he went to say goodbye.

'Take care of yourself, Ash. The sergeant's in a chancey business, too, and one day I may need to rely on you,' she said, clinging to his hand.

The implication in her words put him at a disadvantage. He let her down easy.

'Sergeant Flynn is a tough campaigner, Mary. He'll be here a long time. One of these days you'll have a family. If things go bad for you, look me up. If I'm alive, I'll be on the Wind River.'

Larkin headed for Rock Springs about seventy-five miles east of the fort and reached there after spending the night in the settlement on the Green River. Rock Springs was in the throes of one of its periodic international celebrations. The coal mines and the ranching brought a polyglot population to Rock Springs, immigrants from Finland, Sweden, Poland, and even as far south as Italy and Greece. Ash was swept up into the revelry, which consisted of rock drilling, horse racing, fisticuffs and various other contests of strength and endurance.

Ash inquired around for news of Manuel Elmora and the herd of sheep, and the cattlemen looked at him suspiciously as they denied sighting the herd.

'Dumb as they is, they ain't no fool sheepman stupid enough to come through Rock with a herd of sheep,' was the general opinion.

The news was disquieting, as Ash recalled Thorson's advice to go by way of Rock Springs and then stay east of the Continental Divide. He hoped nothing had happened to the herd so soon. He remained at Rock Springs for a few days and then crossed the Divide at Point of Rocks. The snow was heavier here on the divide than it had been at Togwotee Pass; winter was creeping in. He hoped the Elmoras could get the herd over the divide before it was blocked. Riding down off the Divide onto the high plateau, he stopped off at Rawlins, another coal and livestock camp. Here he could get no further news of Elmora and the herd, so he hung around town under an assumed name, not daring to have his true name connected with inquiries about sheep. Bigge must get no hint of his intentions, and news had a strange way of crossing the wide open spaces on the lips of wandering cowpokes or trappers.

He couldn't hang around without finding some kind of work. Thorson had not staked him to a winter of idleness; just enough to get him to the Uinta Camp to pick up the herd. Manuel Elmora had the expense money for supplies needed to run the herd, and Larkin could not be seen following a herd of sheep. He thought of the two hundred dollars he had paid back to Bigge. He could use it now, but that was the price he had paid for pride, and the price was cheap enough. He got a job on a tipple for a while, where the coal rolled down from the top of the gantry when it was hoisted from the ground. With a bunch of grimy kids, he picked the rock and slag out of the coal as it slid by. It paid a pittance, so he gave it up, pondering the strange quirk of fate that had consigned him to such stupidity. The roundup was over, and there were few riding jobs in the winter. Then he got word of a herd of sheep northeast of town, heading for Bitter Water. As he headed in that direction, he saw the herd from a distance, but he didn't approach the camp until the herd was bedded down for the night. Then he rode to the camp in the dusk. The dogs still remembered him and raised no alarm.

'Hello the camp!' he called as he neared the wagon.

Manuel stuck his head out. 'What you want, *hombre*?'

'It's me, Ash Larkin!'

'*Seguro!*' Manuel exclaimed, recognizing him. '*Saludos, amigo!* You just in time for *cena*.'

'I could use some supper, *amigo*. First I feed my cayuse.'

'The *grano de avena* she ees in the supply wagon, *señor*.'

Ash unsaddled and, tying his horse to the wheel of the supply wagon, fed him a ration of oats in one of the feed bags. Entering the warm camp wagon, he caused a slight congestion until the three of them found a place to perch. Juan was tending the pungent mutton stew and the round loaf of sheepherders' bread. He took the proffered cup of coffee to drink while the supper was cooking, and he watched the lithe, efficient movements of Juan, who presided over the stove. He was a little disturbed that the boy's future should be circumscribed by the life of a sheep camp.

As they ate at the drop-down table, Manuel and Ash using the bed as a bench, they discussed the immediate future. Ash asked when the herd would be sheared.

'We weel not shear all the herd, *amigo*. The first two thousand head you weel take into the Hole, we weel leave on the wool.'

'But what about the lambs? Won't it be hard for them to find the ewes' teats?'

'Nature weel direct them, *señor*. Some of them weel get a knot of wool into their mouth and suck on eet until they starve to death, but not many. We weel keep the tight merino wool on, because eet can stop the bullets, *señor*. Eet ees like the armor, *señor*. Eef we need the protection, we get down among the sheep, savvy?'

'I never thought of that.' Larkin nodded. 'How about the other two thousand head?'

'We weel shear them in Casper; there is a shearing corral there. Many sheep are around Casper; we weel not be noticed among them.'

Larkin slept in the supply wagon, not relishing the frozen ground. He ate a breakfast of sowbelly and eggs and took off across country for Casper. He had time to kill, and he might learn something about the sheep business there. He followed the North Fork of the Platte, stopping off in Alcova, and arrived at Casper by noon the following day. Casper sprawled upon the high plateau, its shearing pens close to the river. Not far off was Fort Casper. He used a new name here, still careful not to let Bigge learn his whereabouts. He checked into the log hotel under the name of Ed Alyard, proclaiming himself a drifter looking for work. It was still two months before the early May shearing season, and Manuel, taking advantage of the browse along the Platte, held his sheep off. Ash took a job driving for the freight line that worked between Casper and Cheyenne. In his off time he sat about the hotel sitting room, listening to the talk of the sheepmen and gleaning what knowledge he could. One day between runs on the freight line, he ran into Juan, who had brought the supply wagon into town for supplies. He felt a lift of his spirits as he saw the boy.

'I'm using a strange name, Juan,' he explained, drawing the boy aside. 'I don't want the name Ash Larkin to be connected with the sheep business in any way.'

Juan nodded. 'I understand,' he said solemnly, his eyes lingering on Ash. Ash learned they were holding the herd near Powder River until the shearing pens opened. He was reluctant to see the lad go, but he didn't want to appear too friendly toward him.

When shearing time did arrive, it was still chilly and blustery, but the sheep had to be separated from their fleece to make the lambing simpler. He got a job at the shearing pens wrangling the sheep through the chutes to the shearing floor, where Indians, *mestizos*, and itinerant shearers separated the blatting sheep from their fleece. The wool came off in one piece like a downy blanket and was rolled up and tied and then tromped into one of the long gunny bags that hung from a frame. When the two thousand sheep of his own herd came in to be sheared, he watched in fascination at the wealth being shorn from their backs. While Manuel brought the herd along slowly toward the Togwotee during the lambing period, Larkin rode on ahead to wait his arrival at Dubois. Now that the showdown was approaching, he felt a new excitement building up inside of him. His whole future and revenge for Virg Culp's death hung on the outcome of the invasion.

He reached Dubois, where he was known, so it was useless to try and hide his identity. He inquired adroitly if a man by the name of Dixon had come through the town, but nobody had heard of him. He wondered if Dixon was having an impossible time trying to find men willing to fight for a sheep outfit. He had one diversion while waiting in

Dubois. Heather Bigge and her brother Robin came to town. Larkin's first impulse was to hide until they left, but a compulsion to talk to Heather forced him into the open.

CHAPTER NINE

'What in the world are you doing here, Ash Larkin?' Heather exclaimed when she saw him.

'I might ask you the same, Heather Bigge,' Ash parried.

'We spent the winter in Denver with my aunt. Pa was afraid the monotony of the Hole during the winter might bestialize us.'

Ash shook his head. 'Not you, Heather. I imagine you're like yore mother was, able to take yore culture with you.' He was thinking of the big house with the pianoforte.

She smiled a wry smile. 'I took my gaucheness with me to Denver.'

'How did you find the fleshpots?'

'Fascinating, vulgar and empty. How did your arm turn out?'

'Well enough.' He flexed it. 'What about Robin's hand?'

'He's still bitter over it. He claims you ruined his life.'

'I lengthened it, mebbe.'

Robin came up behind him. 'I figured

you'd be out of the country long before now, Larkin. Are you sticking around until I get a chance to kill you?'

'Simmer down; I'm here on business.'

'If you're still nursing a grudge against Pa, forget it. He'll smash you. We came by a herd of sheep back yonder. You wouldn't be stupid enough to bring sheep into cattle country?'

'No, Robin, I wouldn't be *stupid* enough. To each his own, I always say.'

'Them sheep are off the regular stinko route. They should have stayed east of the Wind and followed the Powder up through Tensleep. That would have brought them out east of Cody, sheep country,' Robin surmised.

'I wouldn't know.' Ash shrugged. 'I ain't drivin' the herd. How about you havin' dinner with me, Heather?'

Robin let out a mirthless laugh. 'Can you afford cracked lobster, bouillabaisse and champagne? She's got a hunger for them since she went out with our aunt's fancy friends.'

'The fleshpots *did* fascinate you.' Ash grinned.

Heather lifted her chin and gave Robin a cutting look. 'I'll be happy to dine with you, Mister Larkin. Ham and eggs, steak and potatoes, or plain Irish stew with coffee will do nicely.'

Robin chuckled. 'Why don't you ask for mutton and see if he can come up with that?'

'Ain't nothin' wrong with mutton,' Ash parried. 'I had some in Casper.'

'You been in Casper? I thought you smelled funny,' Robin gibed.

'Shut up, Robin!' Heather commanded. 'We came through Casper ourselves.'

'Because it's the regular stage route,' Robin retorted.

Ash changed the subject. 'You stayin' over tonight?'

Heather nodded. 'If we left now, we'd be going up the Togwotee before daylight. The stage won't tackle the pass in the dark with the drifts just breaking up.'

Somehow Larkin had a lift of heart at the knowledge they might spend the evening together. They dined in the café. It was run by a Mexican woman, who greeted them warmly.

'You have the beautiful *esposa, señor*,' she said.

'She's beautiful, Carmelita, but she's not my wife—not yet,' Ash explained.

'Why you wait, *señor*? She is much older than fourteen, the time for *matrimonio*,' Carmelita insisted.

'Fourteen may be the proper age in Mexico, *amiga*—' Larkin grinned—'but here we take more time.'

'*Matrimonio* is one thing the Mexicans do

not put off until *mañana*. Soon she becomes the *solterona*, the old maid. No *hombre* wants the *esposa* old enough to already have three-four keeds.'

Heather laughed. 'We came here to eat, Carmelita, not get a lecture on matrimony. This cowboy has his mind on cows, not women.'

'*Por Dios*, he ees *loco, señorita!*'

'Just feed us, Carmelita,' Ash suggested.

'You need the good *comida, amigo*. Bistek, blood inside; *frijoles* weeth much chili pepper; *pan* weeth *mucho manteca*.'

'Cook the beafsteak so the blood don't drip; not too many peppers in the beans; and we'll butter our own bread. *Comprender?*'

'Cow lover, bah!' Carmelita muttered as she swayed away.

'Why didn't you let her think we were married and avoid the lecture?' Heather teased him.

'Because there ain't no thoroughbred like you mixin' up with a jackass,' Ash said dourly.

'I like jackasses,' she said solemnly. 'They're smarter than they're given credit for, and they're hard workers.'

'This jackass is smart enough to know you ain't goin' settle for a dinky spread with dim prospects after livin' it up in Denver.'

'Why not? Think of the egg money,' she teased. 'I could keep that, couldn't I?'

Ash was uneasy at the turn the conversation was taking. He knew she was funning him, but behind a woman's funning there was usually some deeper motive.

'What is this, a proposal?' he jibed.

Her hazel eyes became dreamy. 'What's wrong with a woman helping a man build if she loves him? All she asks for is tenderness, attention, and the chance to raise a pack of kids.'

'By that time she's hard, wrung out like a bone-dry rag, her dreams suddenly ended an' her soul wonderin' if it was worth it,' Ash said grimly.

'May I speak for the distaff side? She might find satisfaction in the struggle, security in the victory, and the gates of heaven through procreation,' Heather said tartly.

'Let's lay off it, shall we?' Ash suggested. 'It's just a string of words, meanin' nothing as far as you and I are concerned.'

Heather fell silent, but her silence was expressive. She stared at the wall until the arrival of the food jarred her back to reality. They ate hungrily, their young appetites demanding satisfaction.

Then, wisdom giving way to temptation, they walked by the river.

* * *

Boris Bigge paced the parlor of his house on

the island, casting irritated glances on Robin. He had heard the boy's story, but he put little credence in it. Robin had a grudge against Ash Larkin; this could be some far-fetched idea of his to get Larkin in trouble.

'What makes you think there was any connection between Larkin and the herd of sheep?' he demanded of Robin.

'It makes sense, Pa. Larkin has a grudge against you. You know and I know that Mitch Lundy and his men planned the stampede that swallowed up Larkin's herd. Maybe they didn't figure to kill anybody, but they did. Their mistake was that they didn't kill Larkin dead enough. They killed his pal, but Larkin's still alive to bedevil and accuse them. Larkin even seduced Heather; after they ate together, he took her out by the river. She was a changed girl the next morning.'

Bigge's big hands clenched and his lips moved, muttering curses.

'I'll look into the matter, Robin,' he said, staring out of the glass window.

'You'd better call a meeting of the four big ranchers, Pa. They better watch them sheep, and they'd better get Larkin away from the Hole, or *kill* him.'

'Nobody's going to do your work for you, boy. If you want Larkin dead so bad, kill him yourself. I'll handle this matter.'

'If you want, I'll ride to the other ranches

and alert them, Pa.'

'Some day, Robin, you might learn when to press and when to ease up. You might even learn to judge a man before you throw your life away. You're alive now only at Larkin's mercy.'

Bigge himself rode to the other ranches and told what he had heard, but none of them believed the threat was real. The consensus was:

'Larkin ain't a fool. There's no way he can invade us. We'll shoot the sheep, run them over a cliff. If he tries to stop us single-handed, he'll have to suffer the consequences.'

'Not single-handed, Marty,' Bigge reminded Blue. 'He'll have a herder or two and a camp tender with him if he *does* come.'

Marty shrugged. 'They don't count.'

'A man's as big as his gun and as sure as his eye,' Boris intoned.

'And as brave as his guts. Stupidity is contagious, Boris; a man who lives with lions becomes a lion, and a man who lives with sheep becomes a sheep. What do you want me to do?'

'Just be ready in case trouble comes. I'll send a scout out to keep an eye on that herd of sheep. It don't make sense that Larkin is driving stinkos, but he wasn't far ahead of them, according to Robin.'

Bigge visited Mose Kindle of the Lazy-K

and Deno Brandy of the DB spread. He stayed at the DB overnight and rode back to the Big brand a thoughtful man.

CHAPTER TEN

Ash Larkin was having a beer in the Dubois bar. He had been there often enough before to be known to Bill Brady, the owner and barkeep. Brady, smoothing imaginary hair on his bald head, blinked and took the inevitable cigar from between his thick lips.

'There was a man here looking for you, Larkin.'

'Did he give a name?'

'Nope.'

'How was he put together?'

'Kinda tallish, one of them loose, watchful fellers. He said if I saw you to tell you he'd meet with you in the back room around dusk, mebbe six o'clock like,' Brady said.

'Thanks, Bill.' Ash nodded, watching the bubbles burst on his beer. The description fitted Dixon, and the knowledge that the pieces of his plot were falling into place gave Ash a tremor of excitement. During the afternoon he watched the town from behind the hotel curtains which covered the lower half of the windows, hoping to pick out the gunslicks willing to side a sheepman. Some likely prospects appeared, going in and coming out of the stores and bars, but with the transient population going up and down the Wind River, men were hard to classify. A gunfighter could be spotted a block away, but working hands, hiring out their guns not primarily for killing but to prevent killing, did not advertise their trade.

Ash ate supper a little early, and just after six o'clock, he sauntered into the Dubois Bar. Bill Brady, busy with the evening drinkers, looked up and jerked his double-jointed thumb toward the back room when he saw Ash. Catching the signal, Ash went on through the jabbering, smoke-filled room toward the door at the back. Stepping quietly through the door, he saw Dixon sitting at the round, felt-topped card table. A lamp with a smoked chimney dispelled the gathering dusk. With Dixon was a tall, thin man with a flat-crowned hat, who looked out of place in Western clothes.

'So you got here on time,' Ash said by way of welcome.

'Always. I want you to meet Lord Dunsley. He's British,' Dixon added.

Larkin scowled. 'You mean his name's *Lord*, or he's an English *lord*?'

'Both.' Dunsley spoke up in a modulated voice.

'What's he doin' here?' Larkin inquired of Dixon.

Dunsley answered, tipping the hat back off his blond hair. 'I'm a defunct lord, Larkin, destined to roam the earth in search of repentance and adventure. I'm what's commonly called a remittance man—paid by my family to keep out of Jolly Old England.'

'What we need,' Ash said flatly, 'is men handy with guns; men with grudges an' guts, as Thorson put it.'

'Don't judge the merchandise by the looks, old boy. I fought my way through the Crimean War and was in the futility at Balaklava, that comic opera battle. Not all of us were killed in the charge of the light-horse brigade. I was spared, by some irony of Fate, to fight a battle for sheep in God's forgotten wilderness. I like sheep; our estates in England produce champion stock. Sheep give me a measure of nostalgia.'

Ash was silent for a moment, eying the aristocratic man before him. He had heard of remittance men, outcasts from home, who frittered away their monthly stipend on cards, women, or any adventure that might give purpose to their empty lives. He had heard of the light-horse brigade, too, in the Crimean War. Only iron discipline and raw courage could have led men into that suicidal charge, made on mistaken orders.

'I reckon you'll do, Dunsley. This ain't no Balaklava; it's a mite more intimate. Here we see the men we shoot at. Where are the others?'

'I told them to come in the back way, one at a time. We don't want to start no gossip. The herd ain't far from here, Larkin; we don't want to be connected with it too soon,' Dixon said.

Ash had his back to the alley door, and he heard another man enter. The man moved into the lamplight. He was a swarthy man with an inscrutable face and black hair. Even the bulky jacket couldn't disguise his slim hips and broad shoulders.

'Meet Pasco Gomez. He's got a hate for cattlemen. He's part Navajo. The cattlemen slaughtered his sheep, wrecked his hogan and killed his wife on the Shivwits Plateau in Southern Utah. Found him in Indian Territory.'

'*Bienvenida, amigo,*' Ash greeted him. 'This is no grudge fight, but a grudge might spur the action. I gotta grudge of my own. The main idea is to get sheep established around Jackson's Hole.'

For a few minutes they felt each other out like strange dogs getting acquainted. Ash sketched what lay ahead of them. Engrossed in his talk, he did not look up when the alley door opened and another man entered. The man moved into the light, and Ash looked up at him. A strange emotion took hold of Ash, but he beat it back. The man wore a heavy beard that covered most of his thin, flat-paned face. His dark hair hung to the collar of his raw sheepskin coat, which was evidently of Indian handiwork.

'This is Scarface,' Dixon said. 'El Cicatriz, the Indians called him.'

Larkin only half heard what Dixon was saying. He was seeing the man without the beard, a man with a lean, hard face and a stubborn chin. He rose mechanically, kicking his chair behind him, his eyes pinned on the man's face. Then he lunged forward and threw his arms around the man's shoulders, a sob in his voice.

'Good God, Virg, you've come back from the dead!' he croaked.

Virg's arms went about him. 'I wondered how long before you'd recognize me,' Virg chided. 'You're as much a ghost to me as I am to you, pardner. Dixon didn't let on who was bringin' sheep into the Hole. I got a score to settle with Bigge and his men; that's all that drug me here. Now I find *you* bringin' sheep into the Hole. How come?'

'I got a score to settle with Boris Bigge, too, but you've simmered it down some. I was about to avenge yore death. I figgered they had killed you, or you would have been lookin' for me.'

'I owe my life to a Choctaw girl. When I was hit, I passed out but managed to cling to the saddle. My hoss wandered. Finally I lost my strength and fell off the horse. When I came to, I was on a Indian litter bein' dragged across the prairie. I savvy enough Choctaw to know the Indians wanted to leave me behind to die, but Estaviento, which translated East Wind, wouldn't let them. Part of my face was shot away as the slug plowed through it. I've got a scar that needs avengin', I reckon. That's why the beard,' Virg said bitterly.

'I was picked up by trappers more dead than alive and taken to Fort Bridger. I had my own angel of mercy there, the wife of Sergeant Flynn. I reckon we've both come back from the dead.' Larkin sketched his adventures since leaving Bridger, and told how he had resolved to bring sheep into the Hole, to bedevil the cowmen and recoup his own fortune.

They made tentative plans for the invasion. Now that Virg was there, he'd fit in with those plans. Among them they decided to split the herd, taking the two thousand sheared sheep north of the Togwotee because of the mild winter. The herd with the wool on their backs would invade first, browsing their way up the east side of the Winds and keeping off the main trail until they hit the summit. Then they would angle north and settle on the higher bench-land before the cattle ranged that high.

When the meeting was about over, another man came in. He had the look of a trapper. He was a grizzly man, of average height, with baggy pants tucked into his run-over boots. Dixon introduced him as Pierre Delaplain.

'Just about gave up on you, Pierre,' Dixon remarked.

'I stop to argue weeth the stupid *gendarme*. He meestake me for a fugitive, *mes amis*. I, Pierre Delaplain, am the honest man who has the crooked face.'

A gust of laughter greeted this remark, and Ash felt constrained to inquire, 'What makes you so willin' to side a sheepman, Pierre?'

'Because I am a wronged man. Years ago I trap in the Hole before Jackson got there. I was one of the French-Canadians who gave the name to the Trois Tetons, *messieurs*. At one time eet was called Pierre's Hole. I was falsely accused of stealing furs and was keecked out of the trapper village, threatened weeth death if I should return. Now I am return'!'

Larkin looked ruefully over his polyglot crew. Perhaps their varied backgrounds would make them worthy fighters. At least there were enough grudges here to satisfy even Jim Thorson. Not wanting to be seen as a posse, the men left by the back door the way they had come. Larkin was the last to leave, with Virg Culp.

They rendezvoused with the herd east and north of Dubois. To Larkin's surprise, he found that Elmora had hired another crew member at Casper, a tall, bony half-breed with a squaw for a camp tender. The thought of having women mixed up in the fighting disturbed Larkin.

'Squaws are used to battles,' Elmora reassured him.

'What about dogs?'

'Every herder wuth his salt has his own dogs, *amigo*. I hire the extra crew because, when we split the herd into sheared and unsheared, we'll need to have the two crews. This is Longhair and his wife Sparrow.'

Larkin had to agree with that. Then there was the matter of Juan Elmora; the lad didn't appear to be cut out for range fighting. Larkin looked at him in his bulky clothes with his smooth, inscrutable face.

'If there's any fighting, Juan, be sure to find cover,' Ash admonished.

'You think I too weak to fight, *señor*? Sometimes the badger keels the wolf. I was taught by the Indians.'

The boy's reply surprised Larkin, but he didn't push him for details, as there were other things to attend to. The dusty, smelly job of separating the sheep into two herds took the better part of a day. The sheared sheep, to act as a decoy, were to be herded north past the Togwotee to enter the Hole over Purgatory Pass when the time was right. He divided up the men. Culp and Pasco Gomez would go with Longhair and Sparrow. Sparrow little resembled the bird she was named after; she was as solid as an oak and with much the same shape. Delaplain and Lord Dunsley were to go with Larkin and the unsheared herd across the Togwotee. Ash had his misgivings about the motley crew, but it was the kind of crew who just might succeed because of their backgrounds. At the last moment Dixon surprised him.

'Reckon I'll go along with the caper, Larkin. I ain't had much excitement lately,' Dixon opined.

'Danged glad to have you Dixon,' Ash said warmly. 'What made you change yore mind?'

'I didn't change my mind.' Dixon grinned. 'I've got Thorson's bank drafts to finance this caper.'

'The old fox!' Larkin grinned in turn. 'He didn't trust me after all.'

'He trusted you all right; he just didn't trust your youth and inexperience. He doesn't want you to drag him in so deep he can't get out. Men with grudges sometimes find their judgments more hot-headed than cautious.'

Larkin instructed Manuel Elmora to browse the herd of woolies with their lambs, which had grown strong enough to keep up with the herd, up the Togwotee, keeping off the main trails until he reached the summit. Ash decided to ride north with Virg's herd and stop off at his ranch to see how Yancy Kobeck had weathered the winter. He explained to Virg about Yancy staying at the ranch, and Virg applauded the arrangement.

'The old coot's gittin' too old for his diggings anyhow,' Virg opined. 'I'll shore be glad to see him.'

They reminisced about old times and the tricks they had played on Yancy when he had come to visit them. Ash wondered if those times would ever come again. As they neared the ranch in the beautiful rolling foothills, they found the aspens and cottonwoods putting on their new spring finery. Ash loved that country. In all the world, a man finds only one spot he can call home. This was his spot. He was almost ashamed to bring sheep there, but sheep, managed properly, would be an asset to balance off the vagaries of the cattle business. The clutch of pines that hid the ranch house came into view, and they spurred their horses forward. The roof of the barn appeared, and they looked for a spiral of smoke from the chimney of the house. There was no smoke.

'I reckon the old coot is traipsin' off somewhere, mebbe lookin' for gold in the creek.' Ash chuckled.

They rounded the clutch of trees, and the house lay before them. At first Larkin was puzzled, and then a slow dawning of the truth twisted his guts with fury. He lashed his horse into a gallop toward the pile of cold ashes that had once been his home!

'Damn Boris Bigge to hell!' he screamed.

Virg was at his heels, and they both dismounted at once, the completeness of the destruction holding them silent. Nothing stood but the charred remains of a table or a bench and the black hulk of the sheet-iron stove. The fireplace stood like a gaunt specter, overlooking the shambles.

'He burned out a helpless old man,' Virg said in a dead voice.

Another fear struck Larkin. 'He coulda been in there when it burned!' he muttered. 'Boris couldn't buy me out or scare me out, so he burned me out. All the fires of hell wouldn't keep me away from here now.'

'Yancy could've been in there when it burned,' Virg said in the same dead voice.

'Let's find out,' Larkin said, his face blanched with anger.

CHAPTER ELEVEN

Mitch Lundy swished the liquor in his glass and glared at Bigge behind the big desk. Bigge returned the glare. Lundy had come to Bigge's office in the house on the island at Bigge's request, but he wanted to say something as well as listen. Bigge wondered about the rancor in his foreman's manner. He had not been fooled about the hijacking of Larkin's herd and the shooting that followed.

If the shootings had been successful, there would have been no Ash Larkin alive to point the finger at him and his men. He had been too lenient with Lundy. Letting the crew keep whatever strays were picked up on a drive was an invitation to rustling. In a way he was responsible for what had happened, although he had been ignorant of it at the time.

'You tell me,' Bigge said, 'that Tony Salazar crossed the Winds and saw the herd of sheep heading toward the Shoshone country?'

'That's right—a stinkin' herd of woolies. They never been that close to us before.'

'But they're still east of the divide?'

'So what? Do you want to wait until they're crawling down into the Hole? From the story Robin told, I believe Larkin is behind that herd.'

'It always gets around to Larkin, doesn't it?' Bigge jibed. 'He bugs you, doesn't he? Why don't you hunt him down, call him out and kill him?' Bigge suggested.

'I might do just that after what he done to Heather.'

'If he did anything to Heather, he was likely invited. Let me give you a word of advice: be cautious. I saw Larkin in action. Robin's got a grudge against him; he might be using you to settle it.'

Lundy betrayed a sense of uncertainty. He

shoved back his ropy brown hair and ran a hand over his square jaw, keeping his eyes averted.

'How close you goin' to let them stinkos come? You can almost smell 'em now,' Lundy grunted.

'You go to the other ranchers, take Salazar with you. Jeff Alfora can take care of things here, with the help of the *mestizos*. It's our slow season now. I reckon if anybody was going to try for the Hole, they'd do it at roundup time when the crews are on the range. Just to make sure, get two men from each of the other ranches. That should give you a posse of eight men. I've seen fewer men bag a gang of outlaws; you ought to be able to handle a sheepherder and his tender.' There was a note of sarcasm in Bigge's voice.

'If you're thinkin' of that ruckus in Wolf Bait, forget it. I didn't see you winnin' no prizes there,' Lundy retorted. He knew too much about Bigge's dealings to be cowed by his boss.

'If you're thinking of Leffa, forget it.'

Bigge couldn't forget her, though. He needed a woman like Leffa Hanks, a woman who accepted the West on its own terms, without trying to warp and shape it to her needs.

'From what Salazar saw,' Lundy got back to the main point, 'the herd is headed for Purgatory.'

'Thorson could be behind the drive, but I don't think he'd be fool enough to buck the Hole with all the range he's got in the Bitterroots. Did you talk with Heather about Larkin?'

'Boss, it wouldn't do no good. She ain't exactly in favor of your actions. She's like her maw, tough on the outside but soft at the core. I reckon she's already sided Larkin once out of sympathy, just like that old man she's nursin' in the bunkhouse out back.'

'Go do what you have to do.' Bigge shrugged. 'It's a dead to mortal cinch nobody would be fool enough to come across the Togwotee.'

★   ★   ★

Raking over the ashes of the burned house, Ash thought bitterly that he had traded one consuming reason for revenge for another just as demanding. There was no evidence that Yancy had burned with the house. If he had, there would be bones and buttons, teeth or spectacles. Whoever had burned him out must first have driven the old man away. Even Boris Bigge, for all his hard ways, wouldn't have deliberately incinerated a human being. But what about Robin? He was a head-strong kid with poor judgment. The house might have burned while Yancy was away on a trapping or prospecting trip. The thought died a-borning; there, just inside the threshold, overlooked because a charred board had covered it, lay Yancy's pride and joy, one of the new stem-winder gold watches that he had traded a winter's catch of furs for. Kicking the charred board aside, Larkin picked the watch up, brushing the smoke and ashes from its shining hunting case. He snapped open the front of the watch. The cover had preserved the crystal. He snapped open the back and paused, his eyes fastening on the picture of a young woman pressed inside the back cover. Sweetheart? Daughter? Friend? With a grim silent prayer, Ash closed the watch and shoved it into the pocket of his jeans.

'Let's go, Virg,' he said to Culp in a voice made fierce by its very calmness. 'There ain't much more Bigge can do to me now.'

When he finally reached the herd, they were almost to the summit of the mountains and were heading for the defile that would spill them into the Hole. He had parted with Culp at the foot of the mountains, sending him to catch up with Longhair and Gomez, who were working the decoy herd. That left him, Delaplain, Lord Dunsley and Dixon to guard the main herd. Elmora greeted him gravely. 'Thees place ees the deadline, *amigo*. Once across thees *paso*, we are in the land of the *enemigo*. May God spare you.'

'Whatever happens, you and the boy stay

with the camp, Manuel. Keep out of the line of fire,' Larkin admonished. 'Stay with the sheep and run with the sheep if you have to. Where are the three men?'

'Scouting, *señor*. The Eenglish, he go down the pass; the French he go to the north; Meester Dixon he go to the south. He say no shoot, parley first. Stay by the wagon until they come back.'

It irked Ash to have Dixon giving orders on what he considered his own venture, but he knew Dixon was looking out for Thorson's interests. The three scouts returned before sundown.

'We saw no cattlemen on the prowl, Larkin. The high bench where you intend to disperse the herd is free of cattle. The chaparral is pretty thick and dry because of the slight snowfall. It could mean danger if the cattlemen were desperate.'

Ash didn't ask for an explanation. Usually the chaparral budding out with new foliage in the spring retarded a fire, but if it were dry enough it could become a tinderbox. They had to get through the thick chaparral to where the black sage and piñon were scattered, leaving enough browse to satisfy the herd. He felt confident that no cattleman, no range man of any kind would deliberately set fire to the range.

They camped just over the summit, making no outside fire. Juan cooked a savory meal with enough spice to stir the blood in the high cold air. The hot coffee was ambrosia, and the shepherd's bread warm from the oven. Some of them ate in the supply wagon hitched on behind the sheep camp. Larkin was one of those, not wishing to take an advantage because of his position. Dunsley ate there with him. The canvas cover protected them against the biting wind, and they derived some heat from the coal oil lantern between their feet.

'This ain't no place for a picnic,' Larkin remarked, conveying the hot beans and mutton chops to his mouth.

'Reminds me of the Khyber Pass between Peshawar and Kabul. The Khyber was a bit more bloody rugged. I was there after Clive, during the Sepoy rebellion.'

'Yore Lordship, you been quite a traveled man. What was *you* runnin' from?'

'From? Most people run after things,' Dunsley corrected him.

'I reckon it's a mite of both, Your Lordship.'

'Perhaps. Don't call me "Your Lordship." I discovered long ago that my blood is no bluer than that of the lowliest Sepoy. Call me Dunny; my messmates did. Sometimes they called me worse. I was cashiered out of Her Majesty's army.'

'I reckon that's reason enough to put a man on the loose.'

'But I was cashiered for the wrong reason, Larkin old boy. I was young and brash at Oxford and was caught cheating at cards. I had no defense. My family disowned me, so I embraced the army to absolve my crime with blood. It seems I couldn't die, not even at Balaklava. My reputation followed me from England, and so, when my superior officer fudged on his orders and lost a platoon of men, the blame was fastened on me and I let it stay. Now here I am, a remittance man suspect to all and trusted by none.'

'So you hire out to help get sheep on range the cowmen figure is sacred to beef alone. I reckon you got a grudge, but I can't figger what kind.'

'Let's say it's a grudge against society, the establishment order, the bigots who condemn a young man to ostracism because of a foolish mistake, when they indulge in chicanery and license but discreetly, behind closed doors. Somehow cheating breaks a code that has priority over the moral code. But enough of my grievances. What are we going to do about the sheep, old man?'

'We keep moving the herd, hoping to get through the chaparral tomorrow. Then we spread them out beyond the chaparral on that bench where there is fescue, wild peas, black sage and other browse preferred by cattle only when other fodder is all gone.'

The following day they did as Ash had

planned, letting the sheep find their own trails through the high brush. As the weather warmed, the sheep began to shed their wool through a natural process. Clutches of it clung to buckthorn and greasewood. Ash doubted the wisdom of sacrificing the income from the wool for a nebulous protection that might disappear of its own accord. By sundown they were through the chaparral, with no fire and no opposition from Boris Bigge. The lack of opposition worried Larkin somewhat. He said so to Dixon.

'I reckon we covered our tracks pretty good, Larkin. The cattle in the Hole will still be down in the lower country. Maybe Bigge has no idea we're here,' Dixon opined.

'I ain't so sure of that. Robin an' Heather came past the herd on the stage to Dubois. I figger Robin must have mentioned that fact to his pa. Bigge ain't a man to leave any turn unstoned in order to protect his range. The only other thing I figger is that Robin set 'em on the wrong trail by mistake. They could have gone to Purgatory hoping to intercept Virg an' the sheared herd. If so, Virg is in trouble an' here we are unable to help him.'

'It might work out, Larkin. With Virg decoying them off our back, we'll have time to get ourselves established in a defensible position,' Dixon told him.

They made camp on a beautiful upland meadow covered with sage, scrub oak, and

(leave any stone unturned?)

groves of aspen and pines growing at the timberline. The crisp air was fragrant with the smell of pine and sage. Indian paintbrushes, fiery red flowers, poked their faces from beneath bush and bunch grass, while sego lilies turned their fluted cups toward the setting sun. Far across the valley, the mighty Tetons raised their hoary heads like the jagged teeth of a giant wolf etched against the azure blue of the sky. Ash, drinking in the beauty, was startled by Juan Elmora's voice speaking softly beside him.

'Is it not beautiful, *señor*? Why should God make a battleground so much like the heaven?' Juan asked.

'Men make battlegrounds, Juan, not God. Let's pray there won't be no battleground,' Larkin replied, touched by the lad's solemn intensity.

'Then pray, *amigo*, that evil dies this night, that greed is destroyed and that the souls of men are made pure. This I have prayed for often but with meager results,' Juan said.

The boy should have been a priest, Ash thought. His hands were delicate enough to dispense the Eucharist.

'I reckon life's a trail, Juan. If we get enjoyment from it, that's a extra dividend, like a cow birthin' two calves,' Ash philosophized.

The following day, still finding no opposition, they moved the herd across the meadow. By afternoon they came to a small lake, the shore of which was strewn with huge boulders that had sloughed off from the cliff above the lake. Ash rode up to Dixon for a palaver.

'I reckon we ain't goin' to find a much better spot to hold than this one, Dixon. We got water, plenty of browse, an' it's a natural fortification in case of attack.'

Dixon agreed. The sheep were spread out on the rocky terrain, browsing at will instead of running in bunches. For two days they were not molested. Delaplain and Dunsley scouted several miles about the country but saw no sign of cowboys, which confirmed Larkin's suspicion that the men of the Hole must have heard of Virg's herd and be protecting Purgatory. If such were the case, Purgatory could swiftly turn into hell for Virg and his cavvy. Another disquieting thing happened on the third day. Some Shoshone Indians showed up with bundles of wool they had plucked off the chaparral left behind by the shedding sheep. Larkin recognized one of them as Iron Knife, a brother to the chief.

'How,' Ash greeted Iron Knife. 'We are here in peace, Iron Knife.'

'Peace is with us also. We gather only the wool your sheep have left behind. It is not prudent to let the wool go to waste, Larkin. Why you do not shear the flock at the proper time?'

To explain honestly why the herd had not been sheared would create skepticism and a fear of hostilities. 'The pens in Casper were crowded,' Ash temporized. 'We wanted to reach this summer range as soon as possible.'

'But this is not sheep range, Larkin. It has always been for cattle,' Iron Knife said dubiously.

'We are planning to change all that, *amigo*. You are welcome to the wool you have gathered. Your squaws can make many blankets from it.'

The three braves with Iron Knife gathered close. 'But there will be more wool here, Larkin. The sheep are shedding it of their own accord. We will stay and save what we can.'

Ash knew the futility of giving orders to the Indians; they had to be persuaded. He didn't want them here if fighting should break out. If any of them were killed, the Indians would demand satisfaction: a white life for a red life. That might work to his advantage if the Indians placed the blame on Bigge and the other ranchers in the Hole, but he couldn't take that chance. If the Indians became fully aroused, the white men might have to fight together to suppress them. He didn't want a general war.

'Iron Knife, you are disturbing the herd and making the dogs restless. If you go away now, we will give you much wool when we shear the flock at Marty Blue's corrals near his line shack. Take what you have and come back some other time and glean the brush.'

It took considerable argument to get Iron Knife and his braves to leave.

'We Shoshones have kept the peace, Larkin, so we have not been corraled in the Indian Territory with the Cherokee, the Choctaw and the others. We go now. You keep your word, Larkin.'

'You keep your word,' Larkin countered. 'Don't tell nobody you seen us here.'

The encounter added to Larkin's worries. The Indians would have to explain where the wool had come from, and the explanation could not preclude the fact that the wool had come off sheep in Jackson's Hole. At supper Larkin held a powwow with the rest of the scouts and Manuel Elmora.

'We'll all stick to camp tomorrow and see what happens. You, Manuel, move the camp and supply wagon behind those two big rocks near the lake; we don't want to have them catch on fire. We might be attacked in the morning, or at least we might be approached in the early morning. If they want to talk, we'll talk.'

'But eef they prefer to use the gun, *monsieur?*' Delaplain asked in a grim voice.

'Nobody uses a gun until I say so,' Ash reminded them.

'But I came here for the revenge, *monsieur*,

not the *tête-à-tête*,' Delaplain objected.

'You might get yore chance for revenge, Frenchy, but first we let them come to us.'

Ash rode beside Juan as he drove the camp and supply wagons to a place of safety behind the big rocks.

'For no reason whatever get mixed up in the fightin', Juan. You may figger you're a man, but a man don't stop growin' with his years; he keeps on learning in his mind, and that learnin' can win him more battles than bullets.'

'Even a mouse fights when cornered, *amigo*,' Juan said, looking at him with his calm brown eyes.

'You're not a mouse, *muchacho*. A smart man don't get cornered.'

They had an early breakfast, all of them edgy. Now that the time had come to prove their right to part of God's earth, the waiting for action became oppressive. Ash and the scouts rode the perimeter of the camp, rifles loaded in their boots and sixguns flat against their thighs.

It was mid-afternoon when the first signs of hostilities appeared. There was a movement in the juniper and piñon grove that bordered the open ground the sheep were grazing on. Ash saw it first: the high sun glinting off a bright conch or the spurs of a rider. He kept his eyes on the trees as he waved the others to gather close. Men were moving there, undoubtedly angry and insulted that their domain should be invaded so brashly.

As Dunsley and Delaplain drew up, Ash told them, 'Watch the trees. There's men there. Ain't no sense cuttin' up a ruckus till we find out what their intentions are. Where's Dixon?'

'He allowed as how he'd ride on farther an' see what he could scare up,' Delaplain said. 'Thees ees for the action *monsieur?*'

'We'll wait an' see. Let them come to us. Reckon we could use Dixon here right now. I reckon they'll palaver before shootin', leastwise if Bigge has any say about it.'

Larkin had told them about his ranch house being burned out. Delaplain mused, 'A man who weel burn another man's house weel stop at nothing, *Monsieur.*'

Suddenly four men riding abreast came out of the trees.

'Have yore guns ready, but keep yore hands in sight,' Ash cautioned.

The men rode across the open space, spreading out some to present a less concentrated target. Larkin recognized Jeff Alfora and Tony Salazar. His blood boiled at sight of them, but he kept his temper under control. The other two men were strangers, evidently from the other ranches in the Hole. It was a strange confrontation, the three men quietly waiting as the four visitors approached them. When the two parties were but twenty yards apart, the four men stopped, and Salazar spoke for them.

'What the hell do you think you're doin', Larkin?' Salazar said in a flat, even voice that barely crossed the space.

'What does it look like, Tony?'

'Looks like yo're headin' for trouble. No man in his right mind would bring sheep in here,' Salazar said.

'They're not my sheep, Tony. I'm just responsible for 'em. I ain't a man to take responsibility lightly.'

'You'd better take some advice, and not lightly either, Larkin. You got this far 'cause we was fooled by a decoy herd headin' into Shoshone country. The smell of them woolies is makin' me sick to my stomach. Reckon that smell will be around for a long time.'

'It might be here forever, Tony,' Ash said calmly.

'Don't be stupid, Larkin. I was sent here to tell you to take them woolies out the way they come in. You got three days. You don't even make sense, bringin' in a flock of unsheared sheep an' lettin' them molt their wool on the brush. I said three days; that way nobody gets hurt. Bigge's gettin' cautious as he gets older. Three, four years ago, he'd have blasted the herd, the men and whatever into hell-and-gone without no palaver. Three days, Larkin.'

'Was you told what to do in case I said no?'

Larkin's voice was still quiet, but the tension was as taut as a string on a bull-fiddle. One false move, one wrong word, and blood could redden the rocks and brush. The moment of silence stretched to the breaking point.

'*Monsieur*,' Delaplain broke the silence, 'tell them to go to the devil. He would welcome such as they.'

'Bigge has his own plans. We'll be back in three days. If you value your sheep or your lives, you won't be here.'

'This is open range, Salazar. Tell Bigge that. If he tries to chase us off, I'll get the protection of the troops at Fort Bridger. Tell him that.'

'You got a beef with Bigge, Larkin. Settle it with him. No sense in draggin' other men down with you.'

'I ain't draggin' nobody nowhere, Tony. Tell Bigge I'll think on it,' Ash said without humor.

When the four men had gone, Lord Dunsley said, 'What is your strategy now, old man?'

'No strategy. We've got to stand pat or run. No better place than here for the showdown. You men with me?'

'I am weeth you for fighting, *monsieur*, but not for ronning,' Delaplain said, preening his mustache.

Dixon rode in from across the open space. 'I saw it all, Larkin. I figured it might be a good thing to have a man at their rear in case they started anything.'

Dixon was a man of sense and caution. 'Thanks, pardner,' Ash said. 'They'll be back.'

The three tense days were spent in consolidating their position. They kept the camp behind the big rocks, and though they ranged the sheep farther from the bedding grounds, they always returned them to the boulders at night. On the third day Ash was prepared for anything, not knowing how it would go. The answer came just after noon. Ash and his men had dismounted, dallying their horses behind some of the larger rocks for protection in case of shooting. Ash was seated on a rock a little distance from the camp. Suddenly there was the ping of a bullet glancing off the rock on which he sat, followed by the crack of a rifle!

CHAPTER TWELVE

Ash rolled behind the rock and yelled at the others to take cover. Whether the rifleman had meant to kill him or had missed on purpose he didn't know. It could have been luck that had saved him.

More bullets came whining from the trees, smashing into the sheep with dull thuds.

Some of the ewes were knocked over by the impact of the slugs, but the wool that remained on their backs proved a detriment to the bullets. The ewes got up once the shock had worn off. Larkin's men didn't wait for orders. Their rifles began barking to right and left, the slugs whanging into the trees. A man let out a cry of pain in the trees, and a shadow was seen to fall. No one went to his rescue; he was too exposed. He tried to crawl for cover. Then a man rode from the trees, crouched over his saddle, rifle at his hip.

'Come on, *amis*! Let us poosh them into the lake!'

At the same time Pierre Delaplain lurched forward on his bowed legs. 'See me, Jean Villain? I have come back to the Hole! You ron me out; now I will keel *you*!'

Before Ash could shout an order or yell a warning, the duel took place, a duel between two men whose festering differences could only be dissolved in blood. Villain rode like a Cossack, low along his horse's side, wielding his rifle expertly with the butt clamped against his side and his finger on the trigger. Pierre braced himself in the path of the onrushing horse. Villain was shielded by his horse's body, while he fired from under the animal's neck. His first shot missed as Pierre lurched to one side. Then Pierre took deliberate aim and shot the galloping horse squarely between the eyes!

The deliberate execution of the animal left both sides speechless. The horse dropped with the sudden convulsion only a shot to the brain can bring. Villain threw himself clear, sliding forward almost to Pierre's feet, his rifle torn from his hand by the impact. Pierre dropped his own rifle, and as Villain rose to his feet, he was upon him. With a bellow like that of a mating bull, the two men became locked in conflict. There was no squaring off with fists driving like pistons, but close, vicious infighting like that of wolves locked in combat. The two men were locked together by their huge, circling arms, each trying to crush the ribs or break the back of the other. The men in the trees stood exposed, unmindful of their danger, the better to see the conflict. Even Ash Larkin stood up from behind his rock, as did Lord Dunsley and Dixon, the better to view the monumental struggle.

Unable to break the deadlock, the two men sprang apart, and the sun glinted on cold steel. The fighters became gamecocks with deadly spurs slashing for blood. Villain's buckskin jacket was slit from elbow to wrist, and blood made a red pattern as it dripped about him. Pierre was staggered by a thrust of steel between his ribs. As Villain pulled the knife free, blood spurted, but Pierre did not fall. He staggered, but only for a moment. Then he drove in, his knife slitting open

Villain's belly from crotch to breastbone. Villain staggered as his guts oozed out, but the powerful venom that spurs a fighting man drove him forward for one more lunge. Halfway through the lunge, he collapsed and lay quivering on the ground. Like a man composing for sleep, Pierre dropped slowly to his knees and then toppled forward on his face.

The deadly, savage struggle left both sides momentarily paralyzed. Larkin had to shake off physically the paralysis that held him. Disregarding the danger, he stalked out upon the battlefield to claim his man. At the same time a figure emerged from the trees, bent upon a similar errand. The man was Mitch Lundy! The two men met near the fallen fighters; Lundy's flat-paned face like stone and his pale eyes smoky with contained hatred.

Ash said grimly, 'This wasn't our fight, Lundy. It was a feud between the Frenchmen.'

'You may be right, but you triggered it, Larkin. You been triggerin' a lot of things lately. What's to keep me from killin' you right now and sparin' better men?'

'The rifles pointed at you from behind the rocks,' Ash reminded him dryly. 'I brung these woolies in on contract for another man. We ain't askin' for no trouble; just a share of God's earth, a share fit only for sheep.'

'You ain't askin' for trouble?' Lundy exploded. 'You musta been eatin' loco weed, Larkin! Sheep ain't never goin' to get a toehold in the Hole, so get them out of here before worse things happen.'

Just then Delaplain let out a low groan, and Ash's mind was diverted. Delaplain was still alive! He picked the Frenchman up in his long arms and carried him back in the direction of the camp wagon behind the rocks. Lundy, his broad shoulders taut, picked up Villain's body, keeping his eyes off the mutilation and lugged him back toward the trees. Larkin laid Delaplain gently on the ground and unbuttoned his shirt.

'Let me take care of him, Ash,' Juan said. 'I have doctored many sheep torn by the coyote and the wolf. Bring the whiskey bottle from under the bed; you can reach it from the back of the wagon.'

Juan's manner, so self-assured, puzzled Ash, but he did as the boy told him to do. The end-gate on the camp wagon opened from the outside, revealing the space under the slats of the bed. He found the whiskey bottle wrapped in a piece of sheepskin. Juan had torn away the cut shirt, and Delaplain's white skin was exposed, the fiery gash of the knife like blood-red lips. The boy poured some of the whiskey on the wound, and the bite of the alcohol roused the Frenchman to consciousness.

'I weel keel you, Villain,' he mumbled.

'Lie still, Pierre, or you will start the blood to flow,' Juan admonished.

'What we goin' to do with him now, *muchacho*?' Ash asked. 'We got troubles enough.'

'He lost only the blood, Mister Ash. The nights are not so cold now; he can lie under the wagon.'

Dixon and Lord Dunsley came over. 'I reckon the cowboys have given up the fight for the time being,' Dixon said.

'Somebody will come back for Villain's saddle and rifle,' Ash predicted. 'Better bring them into camp. If they want them, they can come there for them.'

Somebody did come for them. Close to sundown, Heather Bigge came riding into camp, leading an extra horse. Ash was surprised but secretly pleased to see her there. Trying to keep his pleasure out of his voice, he remarked, 'You must have rode a far piece at a danged fast clip to make it here by now. Are you frontin' for all the he-men in yore outfit?'

'The men don't know I've come. They talked about getting the saddle and rifle after they had driven you and your stinkos off. I was curious to see what kind of damn fool you're making of yourself now.'

'Look around,' Ash invited, his eyes feasting on her warm beauty.

'I'm looking around. Whatever made you go to these lengths? Sheep!'

'Poverty and ambition, with revenge to sweeten the pot.'

'Revenge! Men spend their lives getting revenge for petty things, letting love and prosperity pass them by,' she taunted.

'Stealing my herd of cows, letting me think my partner was murdered, burning my ranch house with a lonely old man inside—do you call them petty things?'

Before she could answer, Lord Dunsley rode up to them, doffing his hat and bowing gallantly.

'Will miracles never cease? Athena materializing in the wilderness!' he applauded her beauty.

'Not Athena, but Thetis, about to dip this Achilles here in the river Styx to make him invulnerable.'

'This time, don't forget his heel.' Dunsley smiled.

'This is Lord Dunsley, Heather. She's Bigge's daughter. Her mother was a educated, refined woman.' Larkin looked at Dunsley.

'Here? In this rugged country?'

Heather answered his question. 'It's a long story, Lord Dunsley. I might ask what you're doing here.'

'Another long story. Sometime we'll have

to get together and swap yarns, as they say in the West.'

Ash felt uneasy at Dunsley's sudden interest in the girl. A remittance man was usually poor material with which to form a lasting alliance.

'You ain't goin' to make it home before dark if you don't get goin' now,' Ash reminded Heather.

'Thanks for your kind interest in me, sir. I thought I might sleep out tonight. I don't often get the chance,' Heather said with a lift of her cleft chin.

'Here?' Ash queried.

'Why not here? You'd protect me, wouldn't you?'

It ended with Heather staying for supper, which they ate sitting cross-legged on the ground around a blazing fire. Juan was delighted with the company and outdid himself with the simple fare. Heather insisted on taking food to Delaplain in the supply wagon.

'Your friend isn't doing so good, Ash. He needs better care,' she said when she returned to the fire.

'Those French Canadians don't die easy,' Ash reassured her.

Juan offered to give Heather his bed, but she declined. 'It's a balmy summer night. I prefer to lie in the open and study the stars.'

In the morning, Delaplain was feverish, staring at Ash and Heather with vacant, shiny eyes. Larkin realized that the wounded man needed more care than he could get at the camp. After breakfast, Heather insisted they cut some long aspen poles and make a litter with a blanket which was swung between her two horses in tandem. The poles were lashed to her saddle and Villain's saddle, which she was returning to the Big brand. When she was ready to go, Dunsley mounted and rode alongside her.

'I shall see you safely home, Miss Heather,' he said, doffing his hat.

Heather made no objection. 'You can ride Villain's saddle and keep the rear horse steady. Tie your horse on behind.'

Ash watched them go.

There was no attack that day, and when Dunsley returned in the morning, he brought some startling news. Skillet Glacier, because of the mild winter, had busted loose with a record thaw that had sent flood waters rushing into the valley, raising the water of the lake faster than the Mad River could drain them off. The river itself became a roaring deluge, overflowing its sides and flooding the meadows along its banks, destroying the wild hay.

'It hit them very suddenly,' Dunsley explained. 'Every man in the Hole is out trying to divert the waters before even Bigge's home ranch on the island is under water.'

To Larkin, the news was a welcome

respite. 'It'll give me time to drive down to Wolf Bait, load up supplies an' get us a man to take Delaplain's place.'

It took Ash a day and a half to make the trip over the rough back roads to the settlement on the Fontenelle. It was the off season, with trail drives just beginning to trickle through, and a few small wagon trains making their way over Alpine Pass to Idaho Falls and the gold country in the Coeur D'Alenes. Larkin stopped first at Vera Rand's shop and surprised her marking off the days on a calendar which she quickly hid under the counter. The slight flush on her face told him it was a private affair, so he made no mention of it.

'Hi, Vera. You're one of the best-lookin' women this side of the Mississip. Why don't you get out of this raggy town?'

'And leave it more raggy?' she retorted.

'I hope Michele had the sense to leave this place to make her life somewhere else.'

Then he heard a voice behind him, a low, throaty voice sparked with emotion.

'What do you mean—I had sense enough to leave town? I had sense enough to stay and prove to the people who know me that I haven't anything to be ashamed of. You've condemned me, I know that. I expect no forgiveness from *you*!'

Ash turned and saw a changed Michele Turner, the come-hither look gone from her dark eyes. Her smooth skin was innocent of rouge, and her black hair was pulled demurely back from her face and wound into a bun at the nape of her neck. The white dress covering her bosom contrasted pleasantly with the smooth ivory texture of her skin.

'Mike, you've changed,' he said softly, his voice conveying his approval of the change. 'I stand convicted on all counts but one. You're still the girl who took a beating on my account. That leaves a man with no valid goods to barter with. He's got only one way to make restitution.'

'Sure, I know—kill the man who beat me. Then you might as well beat or kill me yourself. I want no onus of murder on my soul because of bruises that have healed. Can't you see the beating was a favor? Or don't you notice that I've changed?'

Ash swallowed hard. He could see the change in her only too well, but she had put herself out of his reach. She had as much as declared herself a pawn for Mitch Lundy's safety.

'I've told you you've changed, Mike. You're a woman any man would be glad to have as a partner,' Ash said.

Vera shook her head. 'Ash, your feet are plenty big, but you still manage to get them in your mouth. Couldn't you have said *wife*? A woman can take a beating, maybe secretly enjoying it because it stemmed from love. She can take poverty and glory in the pain of birthing, but indifference is the most deadly torture of all.'

'Whoa!' Ash protested. 'Are you talkin' from experience, Vera?'

Vera's face lost its color, and her eyes closed. 'I'm talking from a woman's heart,' she said softly. She forced brightness in her voice. 'Come to supper tonight, Ash; we'll find pleasanter things to talk about.'

Ash told them about his range troubles and the fight of the Frenchmen. He told them about the floods in the Hole keeping the ranchers off his neck. When he left, he went to Blacky Brown's cabin, hoping to enlist him in Pierre's place. Blacky was a friend of Thorson, and it was he who had suggested the invasion of the Hole. Men willing to risk their lives for sheep were few, and Blacky seemed a likely choice. When he reached the cabin he found it locked, and it gave the appearance of having been abandoned for some time. He went back uptown to Leffa's bar, hoping she might know where Blacky was. The bar was quiet in mid-afternoon, and he found Gospel McKinley polishing glasses while Cleo, her young face contorted with emotion, was seated on the bar singing a lusty song she had heard in the bar and didn't understand.

'Hello theah, Mistah Larkin,' Gospel

greeted Ash. To Cleo, 'Quit youah caterwaulerin', chile, an' go git you some hymns to sing.'

'How about "Rocky Ages"?' Cleo retorted.

'Git goin' an' tell youah ma an' Miss Leffa that Lahkin's heah.'

'Beulah ain't my ma!'

'She's youah ma now I'm married to her. You remembah that!'

Cleo skipped through the rear door, pigtails flying.

'How are things here, Gospel?' Ash inquired. 'Apart from you gettin' hitched?'

'Quiet. How you makin' out in the Hole? Rumah has it you brung sheep in theah.'

Ash sketched the happenings in the Hole, and Leffa appeared when he had about finished his short recital.

'Come back to the living room, Ash,' she greeted him. 'I don't entertain *friends* in the bar.'

'Thanks for the consideration, Leffa, but don't bother over me.'

'You're a fine one to talk about bother. I hear that that's all you're doing up in the Hole—bothering people,' she accused him.

'I only bother 'em when they bother me first.'

'You're not that stupid, and neither am I. You know damned well bringing sheep within smelling distance of Jackson's Hole is an invitation to all-out war. I'm surprised you lasted this long.'

'I've been helped by luck an' nature.' He went on to tell what had happened to him and the herd. Leffa hushed him, insisting on him coming to her living room to finish the conversation. Leffa's tasteful and warm living quarters were a far cry from a sheep camp, and at first Ash felt awkward. Leffa called Beulah and sent her for a bottle and glasses.

'How's Bigge taking all this?' she inquired with concern.

'We had one warnin' an' one confrontation. Now the flood's keepin' 'em all busy; that's how come I'm here. Do you know where Blacky is? I thought he might replace the Frenchman.'

'Blacky goes to Thermopolis twice a year to collect his commissions on the petrolatum the dude is taking out of Blacky's ground. Blacky's doing all right. I'm not sure he'd care to risk his neck nursing woolies.'

'He put me up to the caper.'

'You accepted it; it's yours to finish. How's Heather? Is she still playing the piano and taking in birds with broken wings?'

'She took me in. She's nursing Delaplain, as I said. What do you know about Heather? Has she ever been here?'

'No. Boris got me as far as the Hole once. I stayed at the house a few days, but I was a stranger there. The house still belongs to Lillian, his dead wife. I think he still belongs to her, too, even though he's trying to escape. I wonder if the bear got indigestion?'

'That's a strong thing to say, Leffa, about the dead.'

'That's just it; she's not dead. She's alive in Heather. She's still goading Robin to be more than he is; Boris is still haunted by her aura of superiority. Some day he'll get shocked out of it. I don't know about Heather.'

'I've got a remittance man on my crew, a ne'er-do-well by the name of Lord Dunsley. He made eyes at Heather and went back to the house with her. I hope he don't compromise her.'

'You'd better pity Dunsley,' Leffa said dryly. 'Stay and have supper with us, Ash.'

'I already have an invite from Vera Rand. But thanks; it ain't often a stubborn jackass gets two invites in one day.'

'There must be some good in the stubborn jackass. Just meeting you has made a changed woman out of Michele Turner. She's a good kid.'

'She was always a good kid; I didn't change that. She just took a square look at herself and didn't like what she saw.'

At Vera's, Larkin invaded the kitchen while Vera closed up shop. Michele was presiding very domestically over steaming pots from which came the piquant odors of spices and mysterious vittles hidden by chattering lids. Michele's face was flushed by the steamy heat, giving it an alive, ruddy appearance that accentuated her long dark lashes and moist lips. She was a far cry from the brassy Mike he had known at Leffa's.

'I don't like strange men in my kitchen. Husbands are barely endurable. Go have the drink I set out for you in the living room. Vera will join you; she has no sins to atone for.'

'Low blow, Mike.'

'You ought to know; you're an expert on low blows.'

Her remark struck home, and he went into the living room rather than put his foot in his mouth again.

The dinner was delicious and the conversation free of controversy. When it was over, Vera said, 'Why don't you two go for a walk? It's a beautiful night, balmy and moonlit. Soon the chill will be setting in again.'

Ash welcomed the suggestion. They walked to the chattering waters of the Fontenelle, and Ash recalled the night he had walked with Heather outside of Dubois. He spread his jacket for Michele to sit on and reclined beside her, watching the moonlight dancing on the ripples.

'What now, Mike?' he asked. 'Where do you go from here?'

'I don't know. I've made the break; that's enough for now. The future has a way of confounding our most careful plans. Before I met you, Ash, I had no hope of being what I am now trying to become. I'm sure I shall never go back, but what lies ahead is a murky, indistinct thing.'

And Ash understood that Mitch Lundy stood between them, an obstacle only a miracle could remove.

Three days later, when Larkin returned to camp with the wagonload of provisions, but without a man to replace Delaplain, he was stunned by what he found. Dead sheep were lying about, some with bullet holes in their heads. The camp wagon was partly smashed, one of the wheels askew. The boulders about the lake had multiplied in number. As he drew closer, he saw Dixon and Juan on the opposite side of the wagon, trying to get one of the repaired wheels back on the axle. He breathed a sigh of relief but the relief was short-lived. It appeared a quarter of the herd had been slaughtered during the avalanche of boulders. The attack must have come at night when the sheep were closely bedded down. He saw Dunsley and Manuel Elmora riding among the remains of the herd, and stopping to talk to some Shoshones who were gesticulating toward the slain sheep. Ash stopped the supply wagon near the camp and jumped down.

'What happened, Dixon?' he asked inanely. He could see what had happened.

Dixon's face was a mixture of anger, frustration, and pure hate. 'Somebody blasted off the rim of the cliff during the night. The boulders crashed through the herd, killing at least a quarter of them.'

'Any idea who it was?' Another inane question.

'Sure I have an idea who it was; so do you. But we couldn't go look for them; we've been busy killing the maimed sheep and trying to get the camp fixed to move out of this hell-hole.'

Ash felt a surge of anger, partly at himself. 'I should have knowed better than to set out camp under that ledge. Were you in the wagon when it was hit, Juan?'

Juan hobbled over to him. '*Si, señor*, but I was not harmed.'

'You're limping.'

'Yes, I am limping. I sprained my knee jumping from the wagon.'

'Put a drag under the axle on this side, Dixon, and put the broken wheel in the supply wagon. We'll fix it later. Right now we've got to move out of this spot. I'd better see what Iron Knife and his braves want. They might have seen the buzzard who tromped us.'

CHAPTER THIRTEEN

As Larkin approached the powwow on foot, he had a hunch the Indians had had a scout watching the herd, hoping for just an opportunity as this. Then another thought struck him. The Indians might have caused the avalanche, hoping to gain a supply of meat to jerk and dry for the winter. He doubted it, though, because Indians knew little about blasting. Knives and guns they were familiar with, but the intricacies of placing charges of powder properly to achieve a desired result was beyond them.

'How, Iron Knife,' Ash greeted, raising his hand with the palm down. 'What's goin' on here?'

'These 'Shones want the meat from the sheep,' Dunsley said. 'I tried to barter with them.'

'Barter?' Larkin scowled.

'I asked them to tell us the name of the man who blasted the rocks off the cliff. They evidently were aware of what was happening; they were here chop-chop,' Dunsley said.

Iron Knife said, 'Indian no travel at night. Night is for the spirits.'

'How did you know the sheep had been killed?'

'Indians have long eyes. You give us meat,

we find man who make the mountain break down.'

'That's about the best offer we'll get, Dunny. No use to let the meat spoil; let 'em have it.'

They got the camp wagon so they could move it with a drag under the offside rear wheel, and they started the remainder of the herd north, toward Purgatory. Ash hoped to meet up with Virg and his herd before winter. They left the Indians harvesting the meat and hides, knowing the futility of trying to trace and identify the men who had caused the disaster. In late afternoon, a lone Indian rode into camp, leading a horse with a body lashed across the saddle. It was Iron Knife, who had kept his word, bringing in a suspect. Larkin's blood drained from his face as he recognized the body.

'How,' Iron Knife greeted him. 'I have kept my word. Only one man blow up mountain. Here is that man.'

The name that jerked from Ash's throat was like a sob. 'Robin Bigge!'

'He's not a man; he's a boy,' Dunsley interjected.

'He's Heather's brother; he had a personal grudge against me. I reckon he figgered to make hisself big with the ranchers an' get even with me at the same time. Give me a hand, Dunny.'

Gently they unlashed the body and laid it

on the ground.

'We're even now, Iron Knife. Chief's son has kept his word.'

Ash was startled by Dunsley's exclamation. 'By Jove, he's not entirely gone, Larkin!'

Ash dropped to his knees by Robin's side and put his ear to his mouth. The faint breathing was barely audible. Quickly he felt Robin over but found no bones broken. He noticed the coagulated blood about the boy's head and felt the indentation in his skull.

Ash leaned back. 'He didn't get out of the way of his own blasts,' he said.

'Hoist on his own petard, I'd say,' Dunsley mused.

'We can't treat his head wound here; we might kill him. I'll have to get him home. Washita is the only one who might save him. I reckon she's been gettin' plenty of practice lately. I'll have to take the short way down. It's rough, but the horse's gait will cushion the roughness better than any wagon could on the road.'

'I selected my horse because of his easy gait, Larkin,' Dunsley said. 'Let me take him home.'

'No. I've got to take him. It's a personal thing,' Ash said.

'Then use my horse,' Dunsley offered.

Larkin mounted and had them lift the limp form of Robin up behind him. 'Tie his body tightly to mine so it can't shift.'

When they were lashed together, Ash started off the bench. It was after midnight when he reached the ferry, and he didn't know whether he was carrying a corpse or a live man behind him. There he found another obstacle. The floods had raised the level of the lake until the ferry crossing was useless. The cables had been washed away or submerged. It was impossible for him to dismount, a complication he had not thought of when he started out. He saw a dim light in the trading post on the ledge above the water and hopefully made his way there. Bigge would have a watchman there to prevent pilfering. He rode close to the heavy door of the post and beat upon it with the butt of his gun. He knocked again. After a pause, a brighter light shone in the front window, and the door creaked open. He sat there staring at the disheveled form of Heather Bigge, swaddled in a flannel night shirt. For a moment they eyed each other like two apparitions muted by the confrontation. Heather broke the silence.

'What in the world are you doing here, Ash Larkin?' she asked, holding the lantern higher.

'No time for chit-chat, Heather.' Briefly he told her what had happened. 'I need a man to get Robin off my back. I'm not sure whether he's still alive or not.'

'I'll help you,' Heather offered.

'He's a dead weight. You might let him fall.'

Washita's strong, stoical face swam into the lantern light. 'What is the trouble here? Who rides at night to disturb the spirits of my people?'

Heather explained. 'Get a knife, Washita, so we can cut the ropes; untying them would be too slow and clumsy.'

When they had Robin inside, lying on a new blanket Heather had taken off the shelf, Washita demanded water and whiskey. Ash brought whiskey from the bar at the rear of the building which had been closed for the night. When he returned with the whiskey, Heather, who was tearing up some material for rags, said in a hollow voice, 'He's still alive, but barely.'

'I'm sorry it happened,' Ash said, putting an arm around her shoulder.

She didn't react to the contact. 'He brought it on himself. Pa didn't tell him to blast the cliff. I gave him the powder from the stock here; I thought it was for blasting log jams on the river.'

'Where *is* yore pa?'

'He and the men are camped down-river, trying to save what wild hay they can before it gets mildewed from the water.'

Washita looked up from her ministrations. 'His head very bad. He is with the spirits now, but he still breathes. Perhaps the spirits will let him come back.'

The news was no better and no worse than Ash had expected. 'Where's Delaplain?' he asked Heather.

'He left yesterday, heading for Canada. He said he had had his revenge on the Hole by killing Villain.'

'I didn't get a chance to pay him for his last month.'

'He took provisions here and told me to collect from you,' Heather said.

'You're a trusting soul, Heather. You want yore money now?'

'Forget it. You brought Robin here. Few men would have bothered with him after what he'd done.'

When Ash got ready to ride back to camp, Heather objected. 'You're tuckered out, Ash. You're going to sleep here for the rest of the night. There are plenty of blankets, and Washita can be our chaperone.'

'It could cause more trouble if I'm found here. Some day Lundy's going to try to kill me, and I ain't ready for the showdown just yet,' Ash said. 'Was yore house on the island flooded?'

'No, but it's impossible to get across to it. Pa's got some Indians building us some canoes. There's an old coot over there keeping an eye on things. He wandered in a long time ago; didn't know his own name. Pa let him stay on and do chores. The house is safe, or he'd have sent up a signal smoke. Washita will put your horse up in the shed out back.'

They lay on some grain bags, close enough so they could touch each other, although they did not. Ash, still curious, asked her about Dunsley.

'He come back from yore place a mite subdued. For a remittance man, that's out of character.'

'What's wrong with remittance men?' she retorted.

'Nothin' hard work an' a little poverty can't cure. They take their pleasures where they find them, regardless of hell or heartbreak.'

'Dunsley's a gentleman.'

'How would you know?'

'I've been to Denver, remember? Dunny's the victim of stupid bigotry and misplaced blame. He scoffs at the bigotry, but the blame he assumed to protect another. He needs straightening out.'

'Like your mother straightened out yore father?'

'Go to sleep.'

When Larkin returned to the herd, he was too busy to think of anything but the job ahead of him. They repaired the camp wagon and pushed the sheep north, hoping to find a way to lower country before the hard winter set in. They were still on the benchland when

Virgil Culp met them, driving a small band of bucks.

'It's almost breedin' time, Ash. If you want lambs in May, you gotta breed in the fall. Thorson sent the bucks down through Carter's Hell from the Targhee by prairie schooner. I had to drive 'em over Purgatory.'

After an effusive reunion, they exchanged experiences. Virg told how the ranchers had actually blockaded Purgatory Pass until he had convinced them he wasn't going to cross. Then they disappeared.

'They got wind of me comin' over Togwotee,' Ash explained. He went on to tell of Bigge's orders to get out of the Hole, and of the attack that came when he didn't obey. He told of the Frenchmen's duel and ended up with the dismal story about the bombardment of the boulders.

Virg stayed for two days and then insisted he had to get back. 'The Indians predict a hard winter,' he explained. 'I'll hold my half of the herd on the other side of the Winds near our Puma Valley range. That's next to low country. It usually snows more in the Hole than it does over there.'

'I'll hold what I got left here in the Hole. If I can pull through the winter here, Bigge and the ranchers might cool off by spring.'

They moved on toward a line shack Dixon had seen from a distance in a grove of trees on one of his scouting trips.

'The shack might come in handy if we're

caught in a storm,' Ash explained.

The herd was slowed down by the breeding activities of the flock. The breeding was a most important part of the business. An unbred ewe meant a loss of all the income from the lambs she might have had. Wool and lambs were the answer to all the fuss and bother. Ash woke up one morning to find Lord Dunsley missing from camp. He had a suspicion where Dunsley had gone, but he couldn't decide whether his reaction to the knowledge was resentment or jealousy. Dunsley could have been gone most of the night for all he knew. Perhaps he wouldn't come back at all. The prospects of spending a Wyoming winter out on the range could have been too much for his remittance man's heart. He came back, though, in the afternoon, with three pairs of snowshoes strapped to the back of his saddle.

'Thought we might need these, seeing that the Indians predict a hard winter. One thing I've learned: never dispute the wisdom of a native. These three pairs were all that Heather could spare.'

Ash wondered what else Heather had been able to spare. A few kisses, perhaps? It was useless to scold the Englishman; he was needed on the herd more than ever with Delaplain gone. Dixon pulled out when the breeding was done.

'Thorson expects a full report on how you

made out during the summer. If I leave now, I can make the high passes before the snow sets in,' Dixon opined.

'Ain't time for heavy snow yet.' Larkin shrugged. 'We could still be raided, you know.'

But they weren't raided. Ash got up the morning after Dixon had pulled out and, staring toward the west through the crisp, clear autumn air, saw the angry red and billowing smoke of fire lapping at the feet of the indifferent Tetons. Dunsley was at his shoulder.

'By Jove, Larkin, nature is still on your side. Heather mentioned the fear of forest fires because of the mild winter and lack of rain during the summer. I'm afraid the blighters have more to handle than they care for without bothering with us.'

To Larkin it was a welcome respite. They might still have time to get the herd into lower country without being attacked. Short-handed as he was, an open fight would be a dismal affair. The only thing that could save them now was another act of nature—snow; enough snow to keep the cattlemen busy feeding the cattle and gathering strays. They were almost to the line shack Larkin was aiming for when leaden clouds obscured the sky and the temperature dropped. The warning of the Indians flashed through Ash's mind: a hard winter ahead. As a precaution, he turned the herd toward the thick growths of juniper and piñon nearer to the mountains. He expected no great storm for another month, but if a chinook did blow out of the north, the trees and mountains would afford some protection. They made camp against a cutbank in the side of which were some shallow caves carved by the wind and forgotten floods. Ash had bought extra axes in Wolf Bait, and now he set them to cutting and piling firewood.

'I ain't expectin' too much snow this early, but in case we're snowed in, wood will come in mighty handy. We can always melt snow for water. Manuel, you butcher a couple of lambs; the meat won't spoil in this cold spell. I'll climb the bank an' look around.'

From the bank he tried to locate the line shack, which had been spotted from a distance some time before. He couldn't locate it. The trees were thicker here, and the shack could be hidden by them. He went back and helped Juan transfer what provisions might be spoiled by a freeze from the supply wagon into the camp, where the fire of the stove could keep away the frost. He picked out two of the deepest caves and had their bedrolls put inside. He helped cut and pile wood in the caves and under the wagons. The snow started during the night.

The snow was a silent intruder, with no gusty winds to herald its coming; just an impenetrable veil of large flakes. During the night the dogs, emerging from their blankets of snow, set up a frantic barking. Larkin, aroused by the commotion, rose and went to the mouth of the cave, to be greeted by a blinding wall of white. Far off, the dismal cries of coyotes could be heard, already fretful because of the long winter ahead. Two of the animals, with their yelps and howls, could make themselves sound like a pack of a dozen or more. Larkin went back into the sanctuary of the cave, sanctuary for which he was thankful. Though the cave was not high enough for him to stand upright, it was a protection from the cold air outside and was actually warmed a little by his and Dunsley's body heat. As Ash picked up his rifle, Dunsley stirred.

'That howling sounds like the wolves on the Russian steppes. Vicious creatures. I was once sustained by drinking their blood,' Dunsley mumbled.

'I'll fire a shot or two to scare them away,' Ash said, wondering if Dunny's adventures were true or imagined. When he got outside the cave, he saw the shadow of Manuel in front of the other cave, outlined in the light of the dying fire.

'Put down the rifle, *Señor* Ash. To shoot will only disturb the flock and waken Juan. He will need his strength tomorrow. More better I build up the fire. The lobo he weel not attack tonight. He ees not yet hongry enough to come to the camp of *el Hombre*.'

Ash surrendered to the Basque's greater wisdom, born of a lifetime of experience. He went back inside the cave and pulled the blanket up about him. In the morning the snow was still falling like an implacable barrage of feathers shaken from the pillows of the gods. Now that the crew was down to four men, they all ate in the camp wagon, warmed by the stove and heartened by the hot, spicy beans and the fragrant coffee.

'We must make the flock move, *señores*,' Manuel said. 'They weel remain in one place while the snow comes, not bothering to browse. Later they may need the strength from what they eat now.'

So they tramped through the foot-deep snow, rousing the sheep from their lethargy with the help of the dogs, and seeing that they browsed on the taller black sage and rabbit brush. They eased the herd toward a new bedding ground where the chaparral was well above the snow. Juan had insisted on going with Ash to manage the sheep.

'I need the exercise, Ash. Besides, I love being out in the snow. It's so pure and soft, as though it were covering up the sins of the world,' Juan mused.

The boy should have been a poet, Ash decided, but he concurred with Juan's thought. The snow was a white blanket, protecting the myriad forms of life in their long winter's sleep. By nightfall the snow still fell. They built up the fire in front of the caves, but during the night there was a curious lack of predatory sounds. Ash mentioned this to Manuel in the morning as they watched the relentlessly falling snow.

'You weel find some dead sheep on the edge of the herd, *Señor* Larkin. The lobo is silent when he keels.'

Manuel's observation proved to be true. Ash, trailed by his shadow Juan, found three ravaged carcasses on the edge of the herd. The snow still fell, a mute ghost that promised to immobilize them. There was still browse above the snow, which was now more than eighteen inches deep. The sheep made white furrows wherever they moved. Worried, Ash ranged ahead of the herd, looking for juniper groves from which branches could be cut to provide feed if the brush was totally covered. Some distance ahead of the herd, he spied a grove that would provide feed for some time. They returned to camp, the snow still falling like a persistent shroud.

In the morning the snow still fell, but the air was warmer, which was an added worry. If the snow became wet and heavy, the sheep would not be able to breast it, and if it suddenly froze into a crust of rime, the sheep would be imprisoned as if in a strait-jacket.

The snowshoes Dunsley had brought from the trading post now proved to be a godsend. Manuel had a pair of old snowshoes in the camp wagon, so they were all provided for.

'Lead the horses ahead of the herd, Dunny,' Ash told the Englishman. 'They will break a trail for the sheep. We've got to get 'em to that grove of junipers up ahead before the surface of the snow turns to ice. Me an' Juan will snowshoe on ahead and cut down some of the higher branches of the junipers, the ones the sheep can't reach from the ground. We'll take a sack of meat an' biscuits with us. We might not be back until late.'

Ash and the boy set out toward the north, leaving their web tracks on the virginal snow. They ranged among the trees, heedless of their direction, guided only by the most likely spots in which to ply their axes. Every time they struck a branch with an axe, they were deluged by a barrage of soggy snow. At first they made sport of their predicament.

'Like a snowball fight with invisible kids,' Juan laughed, reveling in the freedom and the bracing air.

They were in a thick growth of trees when the chinook struck. Its instant attack was a swirling, icy gale that carried with it snow as fine as sand and as sharp. The icy particles could cut the skin and blind the eyes.

'Pull yore coat collar over yore face, Juan!' Ash shouted above the din of the gale. 'We got to get out of this pronto! Stay close to me!'

Ash turned in the direction from which they had supposedly come, but there was no landmark to guide him. There was no sun, no moon, no north, no south; only the murky cocoon that spun itself about them. Heads bent, bodies braced, they trudged against the onslaught. The slushy snow that had soaked their clothes was soon frozen, and only the heat of their struggling bodies made it possible to move. Ash kept looking around for Juan. If the boy strayed ten feet away, he could be lost. Ash waited for Juan to come alongside him.

'Give me the sack of food; I'll carry it! Hang onto my coat! Don't get more than two feet away from me!'

Ash felt a knot of panic forming in his breast, but he didn't communicate it to the boy. Their only hope was to keep moving. To stop meant to freeze instantly. To face reality meant instant panic. They struggled forward, heads down against the wind, eyes rimmed with frost. Ash felt a tug at his coat. He turned his head and saw Juan down in the snow. With a harshness born of his own fear, he scolded the boy.

'You've got to keep yore feet spread! Don't stumble over yore own webs!'

'I don't know if I can make it, Ash!'

The boy's words were clawed away by the

wind. Ash jerked him to his feet. There was no place here for tenderness or giving up.

'If we stop we're dead!' he barked.

'We're lost. What difference does it make where we die?'

'Shut up! Save yore breath!'

Ash tried to keep his arm around the boy, to support him, but the snowshoes made that impossible because of the duck-like walk the webs required. He put the boy ahead of him and prodded him forward. Time was forgotten, each hour stretching into an eternity, but in the back of Larkin's brain one thought drove him forward. If they were caught out after nightfall, they would never see the morning. They would be destroyed by the numb, painless death of utter cold. They would be buried by the snow, preserved in their icy sarcophagus until their bodies were found or destroyed by the summer heat. He drove such bitter thoughts from his mind. Juan stumbled again, and Ash helped him up without a word. The swirling fury about them was becoming darker, a harbinger of the hopeless night. The raw will to live instilled in every living thing drove them forward. Then Ash saw a vision; at least he thought it was a vision. The outlines of a cabin loomed before him, half buried in the snow!

CHAPTER FOURTEEN

Ash realized the vision was real. By some quirk of Fate, or driven by a submerged animal instinct, he had come upon the line shack toward which he had been driving the flock of sheep. The snow was three feet deep in front of the door and drifting deeper.

'Thank God!' Ash said fervently.

Juan said nothing; just stood there, staring with frost-rimmed eyes. Ash kicked the door, but it was stuck shut. A blow of his axe forced it open, and they half walked, half fell into the interior. Quickly Ash regained his balance and forced the door shut. Luckily the door was on the leeward side of the house, so the wind was not against it. The blow of the axe had driven loose the rusty nails that had held the keeper into which the wooden bar was shoved, but with his axe he drove the nails back into the log jamb. Then he looked around, numbed by the cold and startled by the stillness within the log walls. The floor was of packed earth, and there was a hole high on one wall which served as a window. In one corner was a bunk on which were piled some buffalo hides and some culled furs left by a previous resident.

Ash knew the danger was not over. Even in the bitter cold, their bodies were slimy with sweat under their heavy clothes. The dampness could freeze the clothes to their bodies unless they acted quickly. There was nothing in the place to burn, even if his lucifers were dry. The only source of life-giving heat were their own bodies.

'Strip off all yore clothes, boy, and get in between those buffalo hides as fast as you can, before the sweat freezes on yore skin. I'll take a look outside and see if I can find some wood.'

Ash went out, making sure the door would open from the outside. He kicked into the snow around the wall but found nothing burnable. He dared not venture out of sight of the cabin for fear he might not find it again. Realizing that minutes counted and that he was in danger of being frozen into his clothes, he went back in the cabin. Juan was already under the hides on the bunk, only his eyes and nose visible. Ash shoved a mangy wolfskin into the hole in the wall. It kept out the blowing snow, but it also kept out the light. There was no time to think of details. Ash shucked off his already stiffening clothing and, groping his way to the bunk, crawled between the buffalo hides and reached for the warmth of Juan's body. The boy moved close to him, trembling as he did so. Ash put his arm around him. To benefit from their body heat, they had to lie tightly together. Then slowly Ash felt a trembling reaction of his own take possession of him. This was no boy who was sharing the warmth of life with him; it was a girl on the verge of womanhood!

Ash was transported by a devouring flood of emotion. He knew now why Juan had had such a subtle attraction for him since the first time they had met. It had been the instinct of nature that had made the boy seem saintly and special to him.

'Why didn't you tell me before, Juan?'

'It's not Juan—it's Juanita,' she whispered, her lips against his hairy chest. 'I'm an outcast from the Blackfeet. I was sold cheap to Manuel because I wouldn't submit to the chief's son. I went as a boy, because as a woman I am not good enough even for an Indian.'

'Hush.' Ash's voice was a sob strangled by his emotions. He dared not move away from her and break the flow of warmth that nourished them both. To stay so close to her could lead only to one thing.

Thus they came together.

Finally Ash said softly, 'I love you, Juanita. If we get out of this alive, we'll be married.'

'We are already married, Ash. Our bodies have completed a ceremony far beyond the words a priest can say. I have loved you a long time, but I am not worthy of you.'

Before Ash could answer, exhaustion of body and emotion lulled them into a dreamless sleep.

When Ash awoke, he was startled by his surroundings. The wolfskin had blown partly out of the hole in the wall, letting in a dim light. Then he felt the warm body pressing against him, and the night before came flooding back to his mind. He couldn't lie there complacently with the warm body of Juanita pressed against him. Outside, the wind still blew, though with abated force. Inside of him his emotions were in a state of flux, but strangely absent was any feeling of remorse for what had happened. It had happened too naturally to be questioned. He stared about in the murky light and studied the double bunk above them. There were slats there, holding the pine twigs that made the mattress. The upper bunk was supported by posts from the floor and fastened to the wall with a wooden cleat spiked against the log wall. If he could dismantle the bunk, he could make a fire on the dirt floor. The bed was a warm nest in which Juanita could keep warm until he had the fire going.

He managed to slide out of bed and wind a buffalo robe about him before the cold penetrated his flesh. Juanita stirred and looked up at him with shiny eyes.

'Don't leave me, Ash,' she pleaded.

'Put yore head under the robe, Juan.' He lapsed into her boy's name unconsciously. 'I'm going to tear down the upper bunk.'

He piled more skins on Juanita and set to work. Luckily, the pine branches that made the bed above were dry. He piled some of them on the floor and, fishing a tin of lucifers out of his frozen clothes, set them on fire. The smoke drifted out of the hole in the wall, teepee style. He laid their clothes close to the blaze and set to work on the bunk. It was almost impossible to wield the axe and keep the buffalo robe about him. He managed to remove the slats from the bunk and added them to the fire. The thick log walls, which had been chinked with mud and buffalo dung, held in the heat. Ash crouched by the blessed fire, drying his clothing one piece at a time, underwear first.

'I'm smothering,' Juanita protested from her nest.

'Put yore head out an' breathe. I gotta get some of my clothes on before I can chop down the upper bunk.'

When his long wool underwear was warm and dry, he slipped it on without looking toward the girl. His boots were still cold and stiff, but he warmed his heavy socks and used them to protect his almost frozen feet. Then he attacked the bunk while the rest of their clothes dried out. Soon he had a crisp fire going, not large enough to fill the room with smoke, but adequate to heat the interior in spite of the open hole in the wall.

'Here,' he told her, 'yore underwear an'

socks are warm. Put them on under the hides; they'll keep you warm.'

Her white arm reached out and took the garments. 'Do you despise me this morning, Ash?' she asked meekly.

'I love you, Juanita.'

'But you left my side quickly.'

'Because I couldn't trust myself. What we did last night was beautiful; let's not spoil it.'

He thawed out the food as Juanita got out of the bed and put on the rest of her warm, dry clothing. They were pensively silent but with an awareness of each other that was electric. They ate sparingly of the food, not knowing how long they might be marooned. Ash dragged the mangy furs from under the bunk and, to his surprise, found a food box. He pried open the lid on its rusty hinges and found a quantity of flour, some dried beans and a tin of salt.

'Provisions from the Lord, who takes care of shepherds,' Juanita said with a lift of her spirits.

Ash also found a tin can under the bunk. With his sheepskin coat buckled about his face, he opened the door, expecting to go out and fill the can with snow to melt for water. When the door swung open, he was confronted by a wall of white. The snow had drifted almost to the top of the door. He dug a can full of snow from the white wall and melted it near the fire. So they were warm and provided for at the moment, but the storm raged on. Ash removed the wolf pelt completely from the hole in the wall so the smoke had free access to the outside. The wind had shifted so that it blew away from the house on the side of the hole, causing a suction that eliminated most of the smoke. Fully clothed, Ash tried to revert to their roles of man and boy, but with little success. He kept busy and he kept Juanita busy. Their dwindling supply of fuel had to be conserved.

Preparing for a long stay, Ash had Juanita make two pads near the fire out of the mangy hides that were so old they had lost their odor. Then he carefully dismantled the lower bunk, cutting the wood into short lengths to prolong the supply. Twice he tried to break through the drift that clogged the door, but he gave up in despair. Juanita mixed flour, water and salt together and, using her fingers and hands, formed some thin, flat tortillas which she baked over coals she raked from the fire.

'This I learned from the Blackfeet,' she said with a touch of pride.

That night they slept on separate pads near the small fire, keeping on most of their clothes to conserve what heat they could. Ash had some trouble getting to sleep, thinking of the girl so close to him. He would ask Manuel for her hand, and they would be married by the first padre they came across. He was startled to hear Juanita's soft voice.

'Ash, I love you.'

'I love you, Juanita. Go to sleep; we'll need our strength in the morning. This storm ain't goin' to last forever.'

The blizzard ended during the night as suddenly as it had begun. During the past forty-eight hours Ash had given thought only to survival, but when the storm abated he began to think of Dunsley, Manuel and the herd of sheep. His bold adventure had ended in disaster. He realized the cattlemen were no better off. They were not only plagued by the winter, but they had been harassed by fire and flood during the summer. He doubted that any of the sheep could be saved. With one of the slats from the bed, he dug his way out of the door. He gave Juanita last minute instructions.

'You stay here until I get back. You've got food and wood for another day or so.'

'I want to be with you, Ash,' she said gravely.

'I'll feel better knowing you're safe here. I'm leaving you my rifle.'

'What for?'

'Hungry wolves can claw and chew the door down once they smell food.'

He kissed her goodbye, and the feel of her lips brought back that first night in the cabin like a poignant dream. For the time being that dream must be kept locked in his heart.

He climbed to the surface of the snow, put on his webs and started out. The brilliant sunlight glinting off the snow threatened to blind him. It was easy to find his direction now, and in an amazingly short time he came to the cedar grove where he and Juan had chopped down the branches. They had indeed been traveling in circles. He saw the sheep floundering in the two-feet deep snow, unable or unwilling to move about for food. He saw Manuel and Dunsley dragging cedar branches to the sheep and breaking trails with their horses.

'By Jove!' Dunsley exclaimed, 'I was about to go out and search for you. Where's the boy? Is he all right?'

Quickly Ash related what had happened to him and Juan, omitting the episode in the cabin. Dunsley didn't question his story, believing Juan was a boy, Manuel's son, but Ash detected a bright, inquiring look in Manuel's eyes.

'I left the boy at the line shack. He's in good shape. How did you make out?'

'We could not move the camp wagon, *señor*.' Manuel shrugged. 'Eet ees snowed under. We walk there at night.'

'If we can get the flock out of this deep snow and over near the line shack, we can use that for our headquarters until the worst of the winter is over. To get the sheep to the low country now would do little good, as the snow is just as deep there, with no high browse. If we stay up here in the juniper groves, we can pull some of them through on branches and berries.'

They worked all day breaking trails, pushing, dragging, chasing sheep out of the deep snow to the ridge where the wind had blown the snow away. The sun warmed and began to thaw the snow. Ash sent Dunsley to pack what supplies he could from the camp wagon to the line shack, and he and Manuel were alone with the flock.

'You found her secret, did you not, *Señor* Ash?' Manuel asked when they came together.

'Why do you ask that?' Ash hedged.

'Because you are a changed man. I see eet in your face.'

Ash confessed what had happened. 'We had no will in the matter, Manuel.'

'I am glad for you, *señor*, and for her. She should know what it ees to be a woman.'

'I intend to marry her.'

'Be not too hasty, son. I feel well to know it was you who have awakened her,' Manuel told him. 'I bought her cheap from the Blackfeet. She would not consent to them, *señor*. They called her "Squaw weeth flat belly."'

'She told me that, Manuel.'

That night the cold clamped down, freezing the rime ice like rock. Dunsley had come back to the herd with one of the horses loaded down with supplies. The cold was intense even before the sun had sunk over the Tetons.

'You take this stuff to the shack and see how the boy is. Manuel and I will spend another night in the camp wagon. If we can get the wheels off, the bed will be resting on the rime ice, and we might drag it to the line shack like a sled.'

Turning aside to Manuel, Ash said hopefully, 'Aren't you coming with me, Manuel?'

Manuel shook his head and said in a low tone, 'No, my son. I would only be in the way. Let her be happy while she may.'

That last statement puzzled Ash, but Manuel walked away without elaborating. Ash reached the line shack when it was nearly dark and had a moment of apprehension when he saw no smoke coming from the hole in the wall. Hurrying into the shack, he found Juanita wrapped in the buffalo hides and the fire nearly out.

'Why haven't you kept up the fire, Juanita?' he asked a little harshly.

'I was saving the wood for you, my brave. I think maybe you not find the herd and we must stay here. Wouldn't you rather have the fire than the warmth of my body?' she chided him.

Ash refused the bait. 'I found the herd.

Tomorrow they will be here, and this will be our camp.'

Ash built up the fire and arranged the two pallets as he had the night before.

'Don't you love me, Ash?' she queried. 'Are you afraid to hold me?'

'It's because I love you, Juanita. When the time is right, I will prove how much I love you.'

He and Juan both went back to the flock in the morning. He had to think of her as Juan. They found Manuel already there, cutting down juniper branches. They moved toward the line shack, and the sheep followed the trail of branches. It was nearly noon when Lord Dunsley came along with the wheelless camp wagon, which slid freely over the hard ice, drawn by the draft horses. By nightfall they had the flock within sight of the shack, and when they reached the shack they found Dunsley had the stove going in the camp wagon and a hot meal prepared.

So they settled there to fight the terrible winter. They kept an ample supply of wood in the shack and under the eaves of the roof near the camp wagon. At Ash's insistence, Juan went back to sleeping in the bed in the wagon, kept warm by the cook stove. He disciplined himself to thinking of Juanita as Juan, the gentle boy, rather than as a soft, yielding woman. There would be time enough for love once they were married and the earth came back to life. True, his emotions were hard to control, and sometimes when they were alone gathering browse for the sheep, he held her in his arms and kissed her, each kiss goading his emotions almost to the breaking point.

The days became a monotonous succession of struggling for feed for the sheep, moving the herd when they could to new feeding grounds. The men took refuge in the shack when the weather outside became unbearable, and the inside of the shack became grimy with the smoke that did not escape from the hole in the wall. They supplemented their supplies with snowshoe rabbits, and the meat of an elk that had come close to camp to display his curiosity. During a January blizzard Juanita became ill. A slow fever had taken hold of her, and at Manuel's insistence she was moved into the shack. The cook stove was taken from the wagon and installed in the shack, the stovepipe carrying the smoke outside and making the shack more livable. Juanita had intermittent fever, and Ash knew that some hidden infection had taken hold of her. There were days of dejection when he saw little sense in holding on. Let the sheep go, let them die! But somehow he could not let go. No matter how many sheep they saved, that number would be doubled if the lambing was successful.

In February a warm chinook wind blew

through the Hole, melting the snow as if by magic, and rivulets of water appeared everywhere. The sage and grass emerged from the white blanket that had covered them, and the sheep ate greedily of the browse. This harbinger of spring was a welcomed respite, and Dunsley helped Manuel move the flock to new feeding grounds, still keeping them among the junipers in case of another storm. But the chinook did little for Juanita, who continued to have intermittent fever. Ash saw the color fade from her cheeks, and he cursed silently in between his prayers for her. He blamed himself for everything, blamed his stubborn pride and his selfish desire for revenge upon the Big brand. Even if spring were to come now, his fight with the cattlemen would continue, and there would still be Mitch Lundy thirsting for his blood.

In spite of Ash's remonstrations, Juanita insisted on doing the cooking and going outside when she needed to. 'Soon the trails will be open,' Ash told her, 'and I'll take you over the pass to Dubois and a doctor.'

She threw her arms about him and raised her hot lips to be kissed. 'Will there also be a preacher there to marry us?' Ash nodded his head in mute assent.

But a cruel and merciless Fate intruded upon his plans. He came back alone from the herd one day to check on Juanita, who had started to take short walks outside near the shack. As he neared the shack door, a man emerged from the trees. At first he couldn't believe his eyes. There before him stood Mitch Lundy, the man he had sworn to kill!

CHAPTER FIFTEEN

Careful with his hands, Ash unbuttoned his coat so his gun would be in the clear. He kept his eyes on Lundy, who had left his horse in the trees and was walking slowly toward him. Lundy's gun was tied down and ready for action, and a mirthless smile flickered across his flat-paned face. His pale eyes were like rivets in their deep sockets.

'What are you doing here, Lundy?' Ash asked, thoughts tumbling in his head. Michele's remark came back to him. If Ash killed Lundy because of the beating he had given her, she didn't want to see him again.

'I heard from a Shoshone scout that you was usin' the line shack. I wanted to pay you a call before I left the country.'

'Left the country?' Ash echoed.

'I'm headin' for Montana. The Hole's about wiped out; there ain't nothin' left to stay for. Me an' you has got a deal to settle. I ain't one to leave no loose ends behind. I reckon at one time you was anxious for my demise. Well, here I am.'

Ash kept his eyes on Lundy's shoulder; the shoulder moved first in a fast draw. Lundy's gun was in the clear, while Ash's was still covered by the skirt of his coat. To brush the skirt back would be tantamount to a draw. To kill Lundy meant giving up Michele's friendship, but then he might never see Michele again. He couldn't stand still for an execution. The icicles were falling from the eaves of the shack with a crashing, tinkly sound.

'When the next icicle falls, make your draw, Larkin!'

Ash tensed. An icicle fell close beside him, and he saw Lundy's shoulder twitch. Lundy had a split-second edge on him because, facing the building, he had seen the icicle start to fall, while Ash was not aware of it until it struck the ground. Ash swept his coat back, and the movement of his coat pushed his gun off center. He made a second grab for it as Lundy's slug tore through the heavy padding of his sheepskin coat. He saw Lundy's finger tensing for a second shot and waited for the blow of the slug. At the same time a shadow flew around the corner of the building.

'Stop! You can't kill him! You can't kill him,' Juanita screamed. She threw herself in front of Ash as Lundy's gun roared. She was knocked backward by the slug, and Ash caught her in his arm. She made a low, mewling sound and went limp against him. Ash was beyond reason then. He let her slide to the wet snow, his eyes fixed on Lundy's shiny belt buckle. Like a man in a trance, he pumped lead at the buckle, unmindful of the bullets that tore at him. The buckle wobbled and started to fall, and he kept pumping lead into the gaping hole where the buckle had been. His gun empty, he dropped upon the still form of Juanita and let the sobs and the tears rip him without mercy. He was still lying there when Manuel and Dunsley, attracted by the shots, came running from the herd.

They helped him inside, and Dunsley undressed him and searched for wounds. There was a welt across his ribs and a flesh wound in his thigh.

'The heavy sheepskin coat saved you, Ash, old boy. I'll have your leg bandaged in no time.'

Ash saw Manuel take one of the blankets and go outside. He was afraid to ask the question uppermost in his mind. The words stuck in his throat. There was no need for the question. Manuel brought in Juanita's body, wrapped in the blanket.

Ash closed his eyes and clenched his fists until the nails bit into the flesh. 'It's my fault,' he croaked. 'All of it's my fault. I've been a curse to everyone who tried to help me!'

Manuel looked at him, compassion in his eyes. 'Deed you make the blizzard to blow, my son? Deed you make the boulders to fall from the cleef? Deed you geeve to Juan the Indian fever, what you call the undulant fever? From eating bad meat with the Blackfeet she get the fever. Sometimes eet goes away for long time, then eet come back again, only worse. What Juan deed he deed; you are not responsible.'

'He was a brave lad, by Jove,' Dunsley remarked.

Dunsley was still ignorant of the fact that Juan was a girl; so let it be. Ash, fighting back the tears, knew he had to let it be, too. It was an episode in his life to be submerged but never completely forgotten.

'We can't dig a grave; the ground's too frozen,' he said dully.

'There is no hurry; the frost is steel weeth us.'

Whether Manuel surmised what would happen, Ash didn't know. The following day some Shoshones came to claim the body. Ash was alone at the shack.

'She must have the Indian burial above the ground so that her soul may rise to the happy hunting grounds and not be imprisoned in the earth,' they told him.

'I ain't got much say in the matter. She belongs to Manuel.'

'We have seen him at the sheep, friend. He has given his consent. After all, she lived most of her life as an Indian. The Shoshone is brother to the Blackfeet.'

To ask them how they knew Juanita was dead would have been futile. He would get the same answer. The Shoshone have long eyes, big ears. So he watched her go, and part of his life went with her, a part that would never be fulfilled. He had to complete the grim tragedy. He dragged Lundy's body into a hollow among the trees and covered it with what stones he could kick loose from the frozen ground.

Two days later Lord Dunsley left camp. 'I'm going to the trading post to see how Heather and her brother made out through the winter. I'll bring back some necessaries for the larder,' he said.

Only Ash and Manuel were left, and Ash wondered how long Manuel would be there. He knew the answer to that; Manuel would die with his flock if necessary. Lord Dunsley didn't return, and they had another heavy snowfall. It meant going back to cutting down juniper branches. The days dragged on, and then another chinook melted the snow, this time with the real breath of spring. With rising hope Ash assessed his losses. They had nearly thirteen hundred sheep left. The new graze would strengthen them fast. If the lamb crop turned out to be good, it would give him as many as three thousand head altogether. He wondered how Virgil had made out with his half of the original herd, or if he had made out at all.

Then one day Virg rode into camp. He was lean and whiskered and hollow-eyed, but he was alive! Ash greeted him like a brother, relieved to know he had weathered the harsh winter.

'We worked our herd down to our ranch. The chicken coop was still snug and warm, and we fixed up the barn to keep the weaker sheep in. The stock of hay we had stacked there helped out. We come through with eighteen hundred head. The snow on the east slope of the Wind River Mountains ain't as heavy as here in the Hole.'

'Virg, you stay here a few days an' help out Manuel. I got to go down and see how Bigge made out.' It wasn't only Bigge he wanted to see; there was also Heather. And he wanted to learn if Robin had survived his ordeal. Dunsley had been gone two weeks, and he never expected to see him again. Remittance men had fiddle feet, dancing to the tune of the will-o'-the-wisp just over the next hill.

At Beaver Dam, he found Bigge behind the counter in the trading post. He was a changed man, the rock hardness gone from his square face. His blue eyes had lost their iciness and regarded Larkin with friendly appraisal.

'Well, I see you made it, boy,' he said quietly.

'We pulled through with better than three thousand head.' He didn't go into details. 'How did the cattle make out?'

'They didn't. The devil rode us all summer, and the hard winter caught us unprepared. The cattle froze, caught in the drifts. They starved because the summer flood ruined most of our hay. Marty Blue an' Mose Kindle have pulled out. I've still got the trading post. The trappers had a good year. The furs were thick on account of the cold, and the animals took any bait without suspicion.'

'How did Robin make out?'

'He didn't. Never regained consciousness.'

'I'm right sorry to hear that.'

'It was his own doing.'

Ash hesitated about asking the next question. 'How's Heather?'

Bigge gave him a queer look. 'Why don't you go down to the house and find out? The ice is still thick enough on the lake to hold you.'

'I'll do that.'

'Before you go, I want to say you taught us cattlemen something. Sheep can take a hard winter where cattle can't, an' they come back fast. I got to build back up again; maybe you and me can work together. Thorson's down at the house. He came to me with a proposition, which included you.'

Larkin, his head spinning at the new turn of events, left his horse in the shed back of the post and walked across the ice to the big house. To his astonishment, the first man he ran into on the island was grizzled old Yancy Kobeck. 'How in God's name did you get here?' he queried.

Yancy, pawing him like a bear, said, 'I was brung in by Indians.'

'Who burned you out?'

'I burned my dang fool self out, son. It was so danged cold one night I put too much wood in the stove an' went to bed. Woke up to find the place burnin' like the fires of hell. I run out an' fell an' hit my haid. Some Indians, attracted by the fire, found me an' brung me to Beaver Dam. At fust I didn't know my own name. Then things got so comfortable hereabouts I played dumb an' stayed on.'

Ash sighed. Pretty soon there wouldn't be anything left for him to get revenge for. Virg was still alive. Yancy had burned himself out. He wondered what he'd find in the house.

'I got yore old turnip of a watch in my bedroll, Yancy. Reckon I'll go inside an' talk to Heather.'

He was greeted in the parlor of the big house by none other than Leffa Hanks. He scowled at this. What was she doing here after so persistently putting Bigge off?

'I expected to see Heather, not you, Leffa,'

was his inane greeting.

'Heather took off with the English dude three days ago. She's taking him to Denver and from there to England to claim his rightful place. She'll do it, too. She's like her mother was.'

'But I don't understand. What are you doing here?'

'All the trouble wasn't on the range, Ash,' she explained. 'Hoskins, in the saddle shop next to my saloon, got his stove too hot. The flue set fire to the roof, and the whole block burned out.'

'You mean Vera Rand's place, too?'

'Right. Vera left town. The man whose picture was on the wall came back. She left with him; he was her husband. I didn't ask where he'd been. I got a hunch he was in prison, but I don't know what for and I never asked. Vera was true to him, that's all I know.'

Ash was afraid to ask about Michele. 'What about Gospel McKinley and Cleo?' he asked, skirting the real question.

'Gospel and Beulah left for Virginia City in Nevada.'

'Did he take Cleo with him?'

'No,' she said flatly, looking him straight in the eye. 'Cleo is my child.'

The truth was like a blow to Larkin, but he soon recovered.

'Don't be shocked. I thought I had crossed

the line until Cleo was born.'

'Is that why you put Bigge off?'

She shook her head. Her angular face was one of the most beautiful he had ever seen. 'Bigge knew about it, but he didn't need me. With Robin and Heather here as constant reminders of their mother, I would have been an interloper. Now he *does* need me; he's alone.'

'I'm happy for you both, Leffa. Bigge won't stay down; he's a strong man and you're a good woman.' Then he managed to dredge up the courage to speak what was foremost on his mind. 'Where did Michele go?'

Michele came in, her hands white with flour. 'Did I hear my name called?'

Within Ash a great metamorphosis took place. The winter of privation and tragedy had given him a deeper understanding of life, one which Michele would comprehend. He went to her like a slightly drunken man, and they embraced each other, flour and all. The kiss they shared was a warm, engulfing thing. There would be time to tell about the killing of Lundy and its reason; time to tell her of his plans for the future. At the moment he savored only the realization of a love that swept away the past for both of them and left the future clean and shining.